JIMMY-THE-ONE

Submariner Sinclair Series
Book Two

John Wingate

SAPERE
BOOKS

JIMMY-THE-ONE

Published by Sapere Books.

20 Windermere Drive, Leeds, England, LS17 7UZ,
United Kingdom

saperebooks.com

ISBN: 978-1-80055-227-2

To
MALCOLM SAVILLE
without whose encouragement and guidance Peter Sinclair would never have told his story.

Many incidents in this book are true. All characters are entirely fictitious, but if anyone who took part in these sterling days should recognise himself, the fact is coincidental and I offer my apologies.

The Author

THE SHIP'S COMPANY OF HIS MAJESTY'S SUBMARINE *RUGGED*

Lieutenant James Croxton, D.S.C., R.N., Commanding Officer

Lieutenant Peter Sinclair, R.N., First Lieutenant

Lieutenant Thomas Benson, R.N.R., Navigating Officer

Sub-Lieutenant Ian Taggart, R.N.V.R., Third Hand

C.P.O. George Withers, Coxswain

C.E.R.A. Reginald Potts, Chief E.R.A.

P.O. Jack Weston, Second Coxswain

P.O. James Haig, P.O. Telegraphist

P.O. Rodney Slater, Torpedo Instructor

E.R.A. Joseph Saunders, Outside E.R.A.

Leading Seaman David Elliott, Higher S/M Detector

Acting Leading Seaman Michael Flint, Leading Torpedoman

Signalman Alec Goddard, Signalman

Able Seaman George Stack, Gunlayer and 'chef'

Ordinary Seaman Tom O'Riley, Ward Room Flunkey

Able Seaman William Hawkins, Seaman

Able Seaman Henry Bowles, Seaman and Trainer

Ordinary Seaman John Smith, T.I.'s Mate

S.P.O. George Hicks, Stoker Petty Officer

Stoker Patrick O'Connor, Stoker

Ordinary Seaman Henry Keating, Telegraphsman and Telephone Operator

COMMANDO

Captain Jan Widdecombe, Army Captain

CHAPTER 1

The New Number One

The battlements of Valletta overshadowed the turquoise deeps of Lazaretto Creek. Across the translucent surface of the water a gaily-painted dhaisa smoothly plied, bearing its cargo of khaki-clad officers from the Submarine Base on Manoel Island. As the crouching dhaisa-man pushed against his oars, he looked anxiously skywards for the expected German fighters, but even they had left Malta alone on this sparkling morning. The dhaisa bumped alongside the stone steps under the Valletta battlements and the four officers jumped out.

Another boat followed shortly afterwards with four more Lieutenants who immediately joined the first group waiting for them by the roadside. A casual observer would have instinctively marked them down as young men, old for their years, and carrying a heavy load of responsibility. Though none of them was over twenty-six years of age, at least half their number looked well in their thirties, and most showed grey streaks about their heads. Even in their khaki shirts and shorts, they had an unconscious air of authority as they strode into the deep gorge which led into the back door of Valletta. 'The Causeway', as the cutting was known, gave sanctuary to hundreds of starving Maltese families who lived in the caves burrowed into the sandstone walls of the sheer precipices. On this hot summer's morning, naked children romped and chased each other through the crowded encampment. Shrieking women scolded their offspring from behind the privacy of crude walls made from sacking, whilst the pervading stench of goats and dirty humanity hung over all.

The Germans and Italians had been bombing them now for nine months. Their stone homes lay about them in ruins, but, here in The Causeway, these families carried on the fight from the depths of their caves. At least they had just enough food, but even now the rats were becoming larger than the cats, and long ago the cabbies' ponies were more useful as meat than as transport.

Gingerly the officers picked their way through this squalid but gallant band of humanity, until they reached a dark tunnel which led to the heavily guarded Headquarters.

"Good morning, gentlemen."

The quiet greeting came from a burly figure sitting across the corner of a deal table. A pointer dangled from his hand and across one wall of the sandstone room was a vast map of the central Mediterranean.

Deep underground and brightly lit by electric lights, this was the Operations Room of the Headquarters in Malta, the nerve centre for all offensive operations against the enemy, and, at the moment, the only effective force in being was The Fighting Tenth, the Tenth Submarine Flotilla.

"Iron Rings again, sir?" laughed a swarthy officer from the group of men which had just entered.

"Yes, Joe, I'm afraid so. But you're one of the lucky ones — you have a train job."

Lieutenant Joe Croxton, D.S.C., Royal Navy, seated himself. As one of the eight Submarine Commanding Officers summoned to this conference, he was Captain of His Majesty's Submarine *Rugged*, and was the senior of the Commanding Officers now settling themselves around the table, because he had carried out fourteen wartime patrols from Malta and had now got his second wind.

The Captain of the Tenth Submarine Flotilla, Captain 'S' as he was known, wasted no time as he stood up to address the expectant circle of Commanding Officers.

"You will all know that the situation in North Africa has now reached a critical stage. While our armies under Generals Alexander and Montgomery are building up their striking power, Rommel has got to make up his mind whether to attack now or never. Through my 'bush telegraph', it seems certain that Rommel intends to attack soon. He is massing in strength south of Mersa Matruh and has demanded all the ammunition and petrol he can get; and, naturally, the enemy are doing everything in their power to deliver the goods. In four days' time, I expect that the Italian Battle Fleet may venture out from its main ports to give full support to their convoys for Benghazi. As you all know from experience, they are sending all they can down the usual routes; from Naples to Tunis and thence by the inshore routes to Benghazi. These are the convoys you have been attacking during the last six weeks. But in four days' time we may expect 'the works'."

Captain 'S' paused and cleared his throat.

"Does General Montgomery know on which flank Rommel is likely to attack, sir?" Joe Croxton interrupted.

"No, Joe, but he'd give his right arm to know."

They all laughed, and 'S' moved nearer to the wall map, his pointer tapping against the outlines of Italy and Sicily. Then he called out the names of four officers.

"You four will form an Iron Ring off your old friend, Cape St. Vito. The Spezia Fleet must pass round there if it is to do any good."

The four officers nodded.

"You three, Harry Arkwright, Bill Hopkins, and Geoff Scatchard, will form a ring round Taranto, here," and he tapped the heel of Italy. His eyes twinkled as he looked at Joe Croxton who was now looking distinctly worried.

"Yes, all right, Joe, I haven't forgotten you!" he laughed, "but you have got a new First Lieutenant for this patrol, haven't you?"

"Yes, sir — Sinclair. John Easton flew home last week for his 'perisher'."

"How do you think Sinclair will cope?"

"All right, sir — I hope!"

Sympathetic laughter from the others brought a smile once more to Joe Croxton's raw-boned face.

"Well," continued 'S', "I'm giving you a train bombardment job to give you and Sinclair a chance to settle down."

Joe Croxton groaned.

"You know how I loathe the gun, sir?"

"Yes, Joe, but Sinclair has had plenty of practice if I remember rightly!"

"You win, sir!" laughed Joe, "but where do I make the Italian trains run late?"

"Here, between Cape Spartivento and the Bay of Squillace," and the pointer once more tapped the map. "You have freedom of action here. Harry Arkwright stopped the Rome Express on the West Coast ten days ago: that line is still blocked, so the Wop is forced to use this mainline route down the South Coast."

"Aye, aye, sir. Any restrictions?"

"No, Joe, you may fire at anything you sight, but you must stop and block the railway line first. The enemy are pouring ammunition down it to Reggio."

"I see, sir."

"Any questions?" Captain 'S' asked while he glanced round his captains.

There was no reply.

"Well, that's all, gentlemen, and I wish I was coming with you."

"You've had your go, sir," laughed Harry Arkwright, and the conference broke up as each officer took his leave.

"You sail tonight at half-hourly intervals. Good luck and good hunting!"

"Thank you, sir."

But Captain 'S' had turned his back, and was already engrossed in further planning.

It was eleven o'clock when Joe Croxton returned to the Submarine Base at Lazaretto on Manoel Island. He wandered down to the bobbing pontoon which ran out to his submarine. Men were still securing her head and stern wires to the buoys, for she had just returned from Torpedo Creek where she had embarked her full outfit of torpedoes and gun ammunition.

Joe watched the spare figure which leant over the side of the bridge to direct operations. It was his new First Lieutenant, Peter Sinclair, recently promoted Lieutenant, and his voice floated calmly across the gap of water, a voice of quiet and unassuming authority.

Joe Croxton smiled to himself. It already seemed a long time since he had asked for Sinclair to relieve John Easton whom he had recommended for a Commanding Officer's qualifying course. Easton had been a good Number One, and they had seen much action together. Perhaps Sinclair had learnt something from Easton? Joe hoped so, for otherwise the next patrol would be the devil. After Sinclair's last escapade, when he had landed in Sicily to rescue Harry Arkwright, Sinclair had developed into a more reserved and tougher personality. Joe had been pleased with him, but a new First Lieutenant was always something of a risk. The troops might not like him, or he might be too lax with discipline. Only time would show.

When Sinclair had been ashore in Sicily, Sub-Lieutenant Tom Benson had taken his place in *Rugged*. Now Benson was also a Lieutenant, and Joe had asked for him to become the new Navigator, because his predecessor, Lieutenant Hickey, had perforce to be relieved since he would have been senior to Sinclair. The new Third Hand and gunnery officer was Sub-Lieutenant Ian Taggart, a sandy-haired Scot from Montrose.

All very complicated, but at least my lower deck is the same. But it's a pretty good team, mused Joe as he watched his new First Lieutenant come striding down the line of bobbing pontoons.

"Hullo, Number One."

Peter Sinclair looked up, his mind entangled with the technical problems of trimming.

"Good morning, sir," and his hand came to the salute.

"How goes it?"

"Ready for patrol, sir. I've just completed with torpedoes, three-inch ammunition and stores."

"Good. Get the confidential books on board. We sail tonight at eight."

Peter Sinclair's eyebrows raised almost imperceptibly.

"Aye, aye, sir. In that case I'll go and get a bath and write some letters," and he saluted before disappearing along the stone-flagged verandah.

Joe smiled to himself, turned away from his beloved submarine lying poised at her buoys, and followed the lithe figure of his new First Lieutenant. *Better do some letter writing yourself*, he thought, *you never know when you'll get another chance.*

At dusk that night the whole flotilla put to sea at half-hourly intervals. Each boat glided silently through the protective boom, to be swallowed up by the gathering darkness as she proceeded down the swept channel round the eastern end of the Island.

On the bridge of *Rugged*, three figures stood huddled in the darkness, stamping their feet in the chill of the night.

"All right, Signalman, down below with you," and Joe Croxton nodded to the slight figure at the after end of the bridge.

"Well, Number One, I hope you've got your trim right. When I did my first Trim Dive as a Number One, we went down like a stone — I'd forgotten the extra ammunition! How do you feel about your first Trim Dive?"

"A bit nervous, sir! There's so much to think of, but I hope it will be all right."

"We shall soon see! Go below and I'll dive the boat."

Peter clambered below and the warmth of the Control Room stopped the butterflies in his stomach.

The klaxon was not sounded for a Trim Dive, but instead the Captain yelled down the conning tower, "Dive, dive, dive!"

Once again Peter Sinclair knew the feeling of responsibility that burdened the mind, the loneliness of authority when a wrong decision may mean oblivion for those who can do nothing but trust.

"Open one and six main vents," Peter heard his voice cutting into the silence.

"Open one and six main vents, sir," repeated Saunders, a quiet Cornishman. He was the Outside E.R.A. and his hands snaked over the panel to pull the main vent levers, and then a dull *thunk! thunk!* was faintly heard from both ends of the boat as she lay stopped and wallowing in the swell.

Peter grasped the ladder for support. He watched the depth gauges, whilst he felt all eyes in the Control Room focused upon him.

But the pointers hung at fifteen feet and the Captain, who had now reached the Control Room, watched from behind Peter's back... Still the pointers hung at fifteen feet. She refused to go down.

"Check one and six main vents," said Peter quietly, while he felt the colour mounting in his cheeks. How absurd not to be able to dive the submarine! He must have got his trim wrong.

"Both main vents checked open, sir," the Outside E.R.A. repeated.

Still no movement of the depth gauge pointers while she wallowed on the surface.

"May I speed up, sir?" Peter asked his Captain anxiously.

"Yes, Number One."

"Group up, half-ahead together," the First Lieutenant ordered.

The brass telegraph handle swung and its bell clanged. The little submarine trembled as she surged ahead under her main electric motors.

"Both planes hard-a-dive," Peter snapped.

Chief Petty Officer George Withers, the grey-haired coxswain on the after-planes, spun his brass handwheel, to be followed immediately by the black-bearded second coxswain on the fore-planes.

Peter's eyes clung to the gauge pointers which had started to move, eighteen — twenty — twenty-two feet.

By speeding up, Peter had managed to force her under, but the Captain could not use the periscope at this speed.

"Stop both," Joe snapped.

The telegraphs rang once more and the trembling in the boat ceased. The pointers started to swing upwards, nineteen — seventeen —

"Can't hold her down, sir," the coxswain murmured quietly to Peter.

"For Pete's sake do something, Number One. We shall be here all night!" the Captain barked. "Put some water in amidships."

Peter felt his face burning with shame — what a start as First Lieutenant! His hand moved upwards to the pump-order instrument. He flicked the knob and a mauve light glowed with the order — 'Flood'.

"Flood 'Q'," Peter ordered calmly. He counted ten.

"Stop flooding 'Q'."

"Stop flooding, sir."

Peter's first Trim Dive took forty minutes. At last the boat was trimmed for periscope depth, not too heavy, not too light, but easily holding her depth when moving at 'slow one' on her main motors.

"Happy now, Number One?" Joe Croxton asked.

"Yes, thank you, sir."

Imperceptible glances crossed the Control Room. It seemed that their new 'Jimmy' had got over his first hurdle. He was 'slow-but-sure' anyway.

"Stand by to surface," the Captain ordered. "Flood 'Q' when I get up."

Five minutes later, H.M. Submarine *Rugged* was on the surface and plugging her way round Malta and Gozo islands.

"Patrol Routine!"

After Peter had finished his supper he wandered through the boat to see that all was well. The red lighting glowed eerily upon the tired men who were already dossing down on the corticene decks. Some were still stowing away their harbour gear and shifting into patrol rig, but in the fore-ends Able Seaman Smith was preparing to go on watch.

"Well, Smith, your 'fish' all ready?" Peter asked.

"Yes, sir."

"Where's Able Seaman Hawkins?"

"He's a lookout on the bridge, sir."

"Thank you. You two are old hands now."

"Yes sir. We're not so green as we used to be!"

Peter spent some time talking to the men on his nightly rounds. He passed through the roar of the Engine Room where the diesels were pouring their lifegiving energy into the batteries, and Chief E.R.A. Reginald Potts grinned at him, shouting above the din.

"Nice to be at sea again, sir!" he said, affectionately patting the gleaming rail which ran alongside his engines.

"Yes, Chief — but I'm afraid I kept you from your supper over my Trim Dive!"

"Not to worry, sir. I've known many a worse Trim Dive!"

"Thank you, Chief. Good night."

"Good night, sir."

Peter went back to the Ward Room. It was good to feel the friendliness all about him. He slipped off his sandals and crawled into his new bunk, which was that reserved for the First Lieutenant. It ran fore and aft against the ship's side and in his imagination he could see John Easton lying there.

A sleepy voice growled from the other bunk. It was Benson, the new Navigator.

"Good night, Number One."

"Good night, Pilot."

Peter smiled contentedly to himself as he rolled into his blankets. So he really was the First Lieutenant — pray God he'd never let them down.

The uneventful passage through the minefields to Cape Spartivento took two days, and *Rugged* surfaced within a mile of the Cape to get in a good night's charge. It was strange to see the enormous radar aerial rotating furiously on the cliff hundreds of feet above them, while, directly beneath the unsuspecting enemy, *Rugged* lay on the surface undetected, her diesels pumping energy into her batteries. As the first streaks of dawn silvered the eastern sky, she slid beneath the waves, and then, six hours later, she was within a mile of the undulating coast, Joe at the foremost periscope.

"The railway line runs along the coast here, Number One. Like to have a look?"

"Thank you, sir."

Peter grasped the periscope handles and was astonished to see that the shore was so close. He could almost heave a brick at that cluster of gleaming white houses nestling at the foot of the little ravine.

"Don't leave the stick up too long. Down periscope," the Captain ordered. He then waited a full minute.

"Up periscope."

The steel tube hissed as it snaked upwards. Peter snapped open the handles and had a quick all-round look before returning to the ravine. His body stiffened.

"There's a puff of black smoke coming down the line, sir," he said as he handed back the periscope. The tell-tale evidence was streaming between a group of green hills.

"You're right, Number One. Take the time, Pilot, and start making a timetable for the Reggio Express."

The Navigator grinned and jotted down the time on the chart table.

Joe steadied the periscope.

"Bearing, THAT…"

"Red two-six, sir," reported the Outside E.R.A., peering at the relative bearing ring on the periscope collar above the crouching figure.

"Three-one-o," the soft Scottish voice of Sub-Lieutenant Ian Taggart reported from the Fruit Machine next to the helmsman.

The periscope handles snapped shut and the glistening tube slid downwards.

Joe was grinning broadly as he turned to Peter.

"The express is crossing over a dirty great viaduct — the tallest, best and most beautiful viaduct you ever did see! We missed it in the sun."

A chuckle passed through the Control Room and the news crackled through the boat like wildfire.

"Let's get in a bit nearer and have a closer look."

The day wore on. The submarine lay concealed within a mile of the viaduct, and, as each express or goods train rumbled north or south, its time was recorded. Apart from a destroyer, which passed well to seaward, and several patrolling aircraft, *Rugged* was undisturbed in her task of compiling a timetable. At night, the glow from the fireboxes heralded the approach of the trains, so that the position and range could be accurately determined.

"We shall have to repeat this for another night, Number One, to make sure that they are running a regular service."

"Yes, sir, and I hope the weather stays fair for our shooting," Peter replied.

So for two long days and nights *Rugged* patrolled backwards and forwards, lying off the viaduct.

"Never knew that trainspotting could be so flippin' boring," complained Smith in the fore-ends.

"Don't worry, me lad, you won't get much sleep tonight," growled Able Seaman Bill Hawkins, a thickset man with startlingly blue eyes beneath a crop of fair hair. After his escapade with Peter Sinclair two months previously, Hawkins' stock had risen considerably in the eyes of his messmates.

"'Ullo! What did I tell you?" Hawkins grunted, as the order percolated through to the fore-ends: "Diving stations in five minutes' time, shift to night lighting. Stand by for gun-action at nine-thirty."

As the red lights were fitted, a dull glow shone eerily upon men's sweating bodies that glistened while they groped for the ammunition in the round hole of the magazine. They passed up the three-inch shells one by one, so that they lay stacked in heaps along the passage leading to the Control Room.

"Diving stations!"

The familiar cry rang through the submarine and men tumbled to their stations, while in the Control Room Joe Croxton crouched over the chart table, pricking off ranges with a pair of dividers. In the last moments of daylight he had fixed the boat's position, so that the gun's crew could find the range on the viaduct as rapidly as possible.

"Ready to surface, sir!"

"Very good, Number One. It's now nine-fifteen. I'll surface and stay trimmed down because we're only a thousand yards from the beach. I want complete silence." The Captain turned towards Sub-Lieutenant Ian Taggart who was leaning against the Fruit Machine. "Sub, pass your orders quietly because I don't want to be heard ashore while we are waiting. I'll give the order to man the gun, and I don't want an infernal clatter before we open fire — understood?"

"Yes, sir." Taggart looked towards his gunlayer, Able Seaman George Stack. The swarthy face grinned from the bulkhead door and nodded.

"I'm going to have a crack at the nine-thirty goods express, Number One. Once the shooting starts anything might happen, so be on your toes," and he turned towards Stack. "Gunlayer, aim at the viaduct, not at the train."

"Aye, aye, sir." The gunlayer rubbed his hands in anticipation.

Joe glanced at the clock. Nine-seventeen.

"Surface!" he snapped.

"Blow one, blow six," Sinclair's calm voice ordered, and air hissed along the high-pressure lines. The boat tilted, the depth-gauge pointers began to swing as she shot from the depths — seventy — fifty — twenty —

"Eighteen feet, sir!" warned the First Lieutenant.

The air rushed upwards as the first clip on the upper lid released the pressure, and then they were up, wallowing on the placid surface.

Joe's muffled voice came down the voicepipe to the Control Room below.

"Run the blowers for five minutes only. Lookouts on the bridge!"

The rustling of Ursula jackets was the only sound to be heard above the whine of the machinery, as the lookouts clambered up the tower.

Nine twenty-three.

"Gun action!"

Sinclair watched the gunlayer and his four men swarm up the ladder, and then the ammunition supply numbers followed them to form a human chain. The gleaming shells were gingerly passed from hand to hand, to disappear into the darkness above.

On the bridge it was very dark. The towering wall of the cliffs loomed over them and a white ribbon gleamed and broke spasmodically along the foreshore as the seas splashed lazily on the sloping beach.

Nine twenty-five.

The Captain was peering over the bridge, binoculars trained high up on the eastern cliff, and then the Sub's voice whispered in the darkness.

"Gunlayer on target, sir. He can see the viaduct. I have given him the central arch as his point of aim."

"Very good. Load with flashless H.E."

"Load with flashless H.E.," Ian Taggart whispered over the side of the bridge.

There was a click as the breech slammed home.

Nine twenty-eight.

"Loaded with H.E., sir," Stack whispered hoarsely from the darkness.

"Keep a good lookout to seaward," Joe Croxton murmured to the lookouts. Then his body stiffened as he bored his eyes into the eyepieces of his binoculars.

"Here she comes, Sub!" he continued. "Stand by!"

"Stand by, sir!"

Even above the slip-slap of the sea on the casing, they could distinctly hear the shrill whistle of a train faintly floating across the water. Stark coughed nervously and Taggart's knuckles gleamed as he clenched his binoculars.

A rosy glow crept into the circle of vision formed by Joe's binoculars; then followed a line of white smoke, red-tinted at the edges from a glowing firebox. Even from this distance he could hear the pounding of the driving wheels as the engine thundered through the gorge and onto the approaches of the viaduct.

"Open fire!" Joe snapped.

"Open fire!" Taggart yelled to the gunlayer.

The gunlayer waited. As his cross-wires swung across the central arch of the viaduct, he squeezed the trigger.

An ear-splitting *crack!* shattered the silence of the night. There was no flash at the gun for they were using flashless cordite, so that their position could remain undetected for as long as possible. But it seemed an eternity before the first shell exploded ashore, a vivid yellow flash bursting at the foot of the central arch, and slightly to the left.

"Up one hundred, right two!" the Sub yelled.

The train was tumbling onto the first span of the viaduct. Joe fingered his glasses impatiently. "Get a move on, for Pete's sake!" he shouted to Taggart.

"Target on!" the gunlayer yelled.

"Open fire!"

Once more the gun barked. All eyes waited for the burst. Then, smack between the spans of the central arch, an orange flash spurted.

"Rapid fire!" Taggart shouted. There was no need to urge on the gun's crew. Bang! crash! bang! crash! the breech opened and shut as the rounds were slammed home.

Even above the pandemonium, the shrieking brakes of the train could be heard. But it was too late. Already the engine was slithering to a halt amidst the dust and debris of the exploding shells. Burst after burst landed squarely on the viaduct, on the parapet and on the railway lines.

The gun's crew was shooting in frenzied haste when a cheer sprang from each man's lips. The last round had finally knocked away the tottering arch and the central span collapsed in a cloud of dust and rubble.

"Well done, keep it up!" Joe yelled at the top of his voice, but then he stopped short. The last round had burst in front of the engine and the resulting disaster was awful to witness. Like a toy train, the engine jumped, hung desperately for a moment, then tottered over the edge of the parapet, dragging its long line of freight coaches after it. Two tiny dots of figures leapt from the cab. Then the string of wagons became wedged, to leave the engine and three coaches dangling over the viaduct, swinging like a pendulum.

"My Gawd!" the horse voice of the gunlayer ejaculated from the smoking gun.

"Cease firing, clear the gun!" Joe barked.

"Check, check, check! Clear the gun," Ian Taggart shouted.

Up the sides of the bridge men scrambled to tumble down into the blackness of the conning tower.

"Sub, go below. Lookouts remain on the bridge. If I'm not mistaken we've stirred up a hornets' nest, so I'm getting out of here. Tell the First Lieutenant to remain at Diving Stations — we may run into trouble!" Joe's voice crackled in the darkness.

"Group up, full ahead together, steer o-six-o."

The Captain hated using the gun and he was glad it was over: torpedoes were more in his line.

The submarine surged ahead through the little white horses that were already playing upon the surface of the sea, for the wind had freshened. Shielded from prying eyes by the loom of the black cliffs, she sped away from the devastation she had caused, away from the scene of her crime.

For Joe was right in his fears; they were soon to pay the price for exposing their position.

CHAPTER 2

The Misfortune of War

By the time that Peter Sinclair stood his watch on the bridge at one in the morning, the weather had deteriorated and a full gale was blowing. But in spite of the driving seas, this was a night of total darkness, one of those Stygian nights that can be felt and which strikes terror inside the ordinary mortal. As Peter ducked from a 'green' sea that swished over him, all he could see above the lip of the bridge were lines of breakers curling down upon him from the unknown, to slither hissing along the gleaming sides of the pressure hull. Peter took over his watch from Benson, the Navigator, who was soaked and only too keen to get below.

Stemming the seas and plugging into the gale, the submarine was almost hove-to, but she slowly increased her distance from her tell-tale position by the viaduct.

Once again Peter screwed up his eyes to peer into the driving spume that lashed the bridge.

Pity we've got to get in our charge, he thought, *otherwise we could dive to get out of this.*

Above the howling of the wind he could only occasionally hear the throaty coughing of the diesel exhausts. The lookouts crouched in dripping misery on either side of the standards, cringing from the sheets of flying water. Peter dashed the rivulets from his streaming forehead, but even now, after only twenty minutes of his watch, he could feel the water seeping past the sodden towel about his neck to trickle coldly down inside his clothes.

Only another hour and a half of this, thought Peter, *and I'll be able...*

Suddenly he froze where he stood. A ghostly shape appeared thirty yards off his port bow, white in the swirling seas and lying low in the water — the stern of an enemy destroyer rolling to the swell. He could plainly see the huddled figure of the depth-charge sentry, lashed to a rail in the lee of the after gun shield, and then in an instant she slipped across the submarine's bows to disappear into the blackness ahead.

"A few seconds in time," Peter whispered, "and she would have sliced us in two."

Then he realised the danger. Supposing the sentry had sighted them?

Peter reeled to the Diving Alarm, and pushed it twice with all his might.

"Clear the bridge!" he yelled to the lookouts. They were slow in getting through the hatch and, as Peter jumped on top of them, the first sea broke over the bridge to send half a ton of water cascading down the conning tower. When he reached the Control Room the Captain was waiting impatiently for him, water swilling about the corticene deck.

"Nearly collided with a destroyer, sir!"

"Are you sure?"

"Yes, sir."

The submarine was already taking up her night-time depth of eighty feet.

"She passed at about twenty yards, sir, but I don't think she saw us in the seas that are running."

"Well, I won't leave it to chance. Any H.E. between right ahead and red five-o, Elliott?"

The Asdic operator was already crouched over his set and listening on that bearing.

"Destroyer H.E. fading rapidly," he reported calmly, "but it's difficult to pick up the bearing with these water noises, sir."

"She may not have seen us then," Joe said. "Steer o-nine-o."

"Steer o-nine-o, sir," the helmsman repeated gruffly as he spun the wheel, for even at eighty feet the submarine was rolling uncomfortably.

"Only another four hours to daylight, Number One. We're about five miles off the beach, so I'll close the coast to try and get in the lee of the headland. I want to get in more of a charge, so, if we are uninterrupted, I'll surface again closer inshore. Go to one hundred and twenty feet to get out of the swell."

Peter took her down.

"One hundred and twenty feet, sir."

Rugged was more comfortable at this depth, but even here she felt the gale. Peter continued his watch in the Control Room and, after surfacing forty-five minutes later, he once more found himself on the bridge.

The gale had already moderated, as so often happens in the Mediterranean, and only a few white horses showed, although a long oily swell remained to remind them of the unpleasant night.

"I'm going below, Number One," Joe said. "Have you got the weight?"

"Yes, sir."

"Good. Call me if the weather deteriorates again, and keep a sharp lookout. We ought to be all right now. We're close in and well under the cliffs."

"Aye, aye, sir."

Once more Peter was on his own. The cliffs loomed over him, gaunt and menacing; he shivered and pulled down his sweater. In each wing of the bridge, the silhouette of the lookout crouched over his binoculars, slowly sweeping his own sector. It was so dark that they had difficulty in picking out the loom of the cliffs from the seaward horizon.

Only another half-hour of my watch, Peter thought cheerfully, as he peered through his binoculars. They were only two miles from the beach, and he could just see a white ribbon of surf gleaming in the blackness. The cloud was still low and it was hard to distinguish the clifftops from the sky.

The submarine slowly zigzagged towards Cape Spartivento, the diesels coughing away happily to give them their vital charge.

The enemy have been curiously quiet, thought Peter, *but I suppose the gale has helped.*

He was sweeping the seaward horizon before returning to landward, so that he had his back to the dark cliffs, Cape Spartivento being two miles distant on *Rugged*'s starboard bow.

Suddenly Peter was blinded. So bright was the whiteness of the light that he thought it was a shell burst. He blinked in the brightness and was surprised to find the vivid light still with him. The starboard lookout had averted his head and was muttering to himself as he shielded his face with one arm.

Peter turned to the source of light. Towards him there curved the dazzling beam of a searchlight, pinpointing the submarine in a blue-white brilliance, so that the shadows of the standards ran darkly across the deck of the bridge.

Peter shook himself and leapt for the diving klaxon.

"Hard-a-port, dive, dive, dive!" he yelled down the voicepipe.

As the lookouts jumped down the conning tower, Peter stood in the glare for a moment, feeling completely naked and blinded by the sudden brilliance. Then a high-pitched whee-ee! fluttered across the bows and an orange flash stabbed the darkness. He could not see the gun-flashes ashore, for the brightness of the beam.

"Not much future in hanging about here," he muttered as he leapt for the hatch. Already the seas were swirling up the conning tower sides as he thankfully pulled the upper lid shut over his head. From the eerie redness below, he heard the Captain giving his staccato orders.

"Eighty feet, steer o-six-o."

Joe was grinning as Peter scrambled out of the canvas trunking at the bottom of the tower.

"Busy night, Number One!"

"Yes, sir, it seems they don't like me!"

"Well, we finished our charge anyway, with only an hour till daylight."

"They definitely had us just then, sir."

"Yes, they know where we are now. Carry out an all-round H.E. sweep, Leading Seaman Elliott."

"Aye, aye, sir."

The Asdic operator crouched over his dials.

"All-round sweep completed, sir. No H.E."

"Good. But I expect they'll be after us — they must be pretty mad by now."

The cracks of exploding shells could still be heard bursting upon the surface overhead. Joe strolled over to the chart.

"Where are we, Pilot?"

Benson indicated the submarine's position.

"All right. I'll keep on this course and cross the river estuary, so look out for your trim, Number One."

"Aye, aye, sir."

"Don't forget," the Captain continued, "if we go through fresh water, we may lose depth rapidly because of the different density."

"Yes, sir," Peter answered, a dim recollection of the hazard flickering across his mind from the days of his training course.

And then it was that all those in the Control Room noticed a sudden stiffening in Elliott's hunched back — a danger signal they now all recognised with the dread and certainty that comes to any hunted quarry.

CHAPTER 3

Cat and Mouse

"Destroyer H.E., Green one-six-o, sir," Elliott drawled quietly. The illuminated dials of his Asdic set glowed dimly from the darkness of his corner in the port quarter of the Control Room.

"Very good, carry on with an all-round sweep."

The Captain strolled to the chart table.

"I'll try to get across this estuary, Number One, before they start their hunt. But I daren't speed up or they'll hear us."

Elliott removed his earphones and turned towards his Captain.

"H.E. increasing, sir. There may be more than one steam-turbine ship, but I can't tell yet. The H.E. is loud and confused."

Joe Croxton glanced at his First Lieutenant.

"Open main vents and shut off from depth-charging, Number One. Silent Routine."

"Aye, aye, sir. Open main vents and shut off from depth-charging. Silent Routine," Peter repeated, and the order was passed quietly through the boat. The steel doors swung silently shut, the black clips flicked home by unseen hands on the far side of the bulkhead. All unnecessary motors were stopped to reduce noise, the lighting was cut down to a minimum to conserve battery power, and men instinctively lowered their voices.

"Half a mile to the estuary, sir," Benson, the Navigator, reported from the chart table.

"Very good, Pilot."

While they approached the fresh water patch, Peter swallowed as he felt the tension mounting. Unconsciously he was flexing his knees to feel the first movement of a bow-down movement.

"Two destroyers' H.E., sir, one Green six-o, the other Green one-two-o. I can just make out their transmission intervals."

"Any idea of range, Elliott?"

"About fifteen hundred yards, sir."

It was this waiting that most men hated because, once the counter-attack had started, they had little time for imagination. Then, from somewhere all around them, a faint 'tick-ticking' seemed to have crept unannounced into their consciousness.

Just like the sound my finger and thumb make when I flick them together, thought Sub-Lieutenant Ian Taggart, the new Third Hand. This was his first patrol and the 'heat' was still a novelty for him although it was soon to become a routine, more dreaded on each occasion.

"Destroyer in contact one-two-o, sir. H.E. increasing."

I never knew you could hear Asdic impulses inside the boat, Taggart thought to himself. *I've got a lot to learn yet.*

Peter stood by his pump-order instrument, his hands on his hips, intent on keeping the trim. He gazed at the depth gauge. Eighty feet: the pointers were steady.

It's lonely here between the gauges, he thought, as he watched the planesmen slowly twirling their brass handwheels — the First Lieutenant's job was a responsible and lonely one.

Then Elliott's voice crackled in the silence.

"Transmission interval decreasing, sir. Range five hundred yards."

The rumble of fast-revving engines, the beating of thrashing screws as the hunter pounded overhead — the noise was overwhelming.

"Starboard ten," Joe ordered quietly.

"Starboard ten, sir."

Saunders, the Outside E.R.A., wheel spanner in hand, slowly stood up from his toolbox and half-faced his panel, ready for all emergencies.

Click-click — click-click-click…

There they go! Peter thought.

It was only when the depth charges were close, that the noise of the depth-charge primers springing home could be heard. Already the charges must be toppling down through the water towards them.

Then an ear-splitting crack squeezed the pressure hull. Men gasped as their tiny world constricted about them, their lungs momentarily crushed by the pressure of the shattering explosion.

Peter grunted and clutched the steel rungs of the ladder, while granules of cork dropped from the deckhead. His eyes were glued to the gauges, where the pointers had slowly begun to move. Imperceptibly the boat slid upwards. Was this just a momentary jolt, or was she being forced upwards by the exploding charges?

"Short and under, I reckon, Number One."

"Yes, sir. She's moving now."

Peter's hands flew to the pump-order instrument. The pointers were moving rapidly now — seventy-three, sixty-eight, sixty feet. The bubbles on the inclinometers had moved backward and the bow-up angle could be felt underfoot.

"Flood Q," Peter snapped, as his fingers flipped the knobs of the pump-order instrument. The mauve letters blinked back at him, 'flooding'. Peter waited impatiently for a check in the boat's leap upwards. No change. Still the pointers flicked round — fifty-eight, fifty-one, forty-five feet.

He kept on flooding — still no halt, as she careered upwards, forced from below by the irresistible force of the explosions. The bow-up angle was acute now and Peter held on tightly to the ladder.

"Don't speed up, Number One. It's daylight now and the swirl will give us away," Joe snapped.

"Aye, aye, sir." He felt all eyes upon him as he wrestled for control. "Hard-a-dive, both planes," he ordered.

Thirty-five, thirty-two — another twelve feet and her standards would break surface — and that would be the end!

"Flood Q!" jerked Peter, using the last resort.

"Thank God," Ian Taggart breathed, "but has he left it too late?"

The Outside E.R.A.'s hand flew to the panel. He snapped open the lever of Q tank, the emergency diving tank which would make the boat ten tons heavier.

Peter swallowed. Had he indeed left it too late? Were they to be sliced wide open by ramming destroyers on this his first and, most probably, his last patrol as First Lieutenant? Once again he had reacted too slowly…

Then suddenly he felt the angle lessen, the boat levelling off from her mad rush upwards.

Twenty-five, twenty-three feet, the rate had lessened.

Twenty-two — twenty-two — twenty-one, only another three feet and the standards would break surface.

Peter gripped the ladder, his knuckles showing white.

Twenty-one, twenty-one, twenty-one, twenty-two, twenty-two, twenty-three — an audible sigh whispered through the Control Room. She was holding, but now came the danger of her stern breaking surface. If her after-ends cocked up too much, they would swirl blackly on the surface.

"Both planes amidships," Peter ordered, his voice steady. The brass handwheels spun.

"Up periscope!"

The Captain uncurled himself from the deck as the after periscope slithered upwards. When the glass broke surface he spun round. He barely had time to sight the enemy before the glass dipped at twenty-five feet and the boat was on her way down again.

Peter held her steady as she dropped like a dead weight. Thirty, thirty-five, forty-eight feet, she plummeted downwards. Gently he allowed the bow-down angle to assert itself and he sighed audibly — a close shave!

"Hope they didn't sight the swirl, Number One. Well done!"

"A near thing, sir," Peter replied, concentrating upon his trimming. "Vent Q inboard!"

The foul air from Q tank roared into the boat, for the tell-tale bubbles could not be allowed to vent to the surface.

"H.E., Red two-o, sir. Running in to attack!" Elliott reported.

"Port ten, steer o-nine-o," Joe ordered, his gangling arms hanging by his side, his shoulders hunched. He was poised upon the balls of his feet, concentrating upon the impending attack.

But Peter's mind was on his trimming. The boat was now hurtling fiercely downwards, with a bow-down angle that became steeper at every second, the pointers racing past forty feet.

"Blow Q! Pump on Q."

The high-pressure air sang as it raced along the pipes to expel the water from Q tank.

Now she'll stop her descent and settle nicely on eighty feet, if I take out as much water from O tank as I put in, Peter thought.

He kept the pump running until he judged that the same quantity of water had been pumped out from O. But the submarine slid quickly past eighty feet to ninety, then to one hundred feet.

Peter, who was wrestling with the trim, barely noticed the next pattern of depth charges which was dropped by the second hunter, as soon as the first had drawn clear. The pattern fell short and caused little anxiety, but both destroyers were still in contact, so *Rugged* could afford to take no risks.

"Shut Main Ballast Kingstons," Peter ordered, for the boat was now slipping well past the hundred-foot mark. Men jumped to turn the large brass wheels which would shut all the main openings in the tanks, and so preserve the pressure hull at these depths. Peter kept the pumps running on Q tank, but, at this depth and at this pressure, little water was being expelled.

"May I speed up, sir?" asked Peter anxiously. "I can't hold her." She was moving faster now, leaping downwards by tens of feet — one hundred and eighty, ninety, two hundred feet.

"No," snapped Joe, "they'll hear us up top. Keep on pumping."

Peter had both planes at hard-a-rise, but they had no effect — still the submarine plunged to destruction.

"H.E. increasing, Red one-one-o, sir, destroyer in contact."

"Very good — report when she gets in to five hundred yards."

"Aye, aye, sir."

From all sides the sound of Asdic impulses ticked remorselessly. Both Peter's and the Captain's eyes were glued on the deep depth gauge — two hundred and thirty feet and only twenty feet to go before she was past her safe diving depth — below that depth nobody knew when the steel hull would disintegrate from the tremendous pressure of the deeps.

"She's bodily heavy, sir. We must have entered the fresh water estuary."

"Yes, and awkward it is too, with our two friends in contact up top. Shut main vents. I shall have to catch a main ballast trim — if I can!"

The main vents thudded.

"Five hundred yards, sir," Elliott reported as the depth showed two hundred and sixty feet.

"I'll take her now, Number One," Joe said quietly.

Plunging to destruction and being accurately depth-charged, there was no more that Peter could do. A pattern directly overhead now and she would be forced down beyond her limit. Peter tried to thrust the hideous picture from his mind, as the destroyer rumbled overhead, drenching them in an avalanche of sound.

"Group up, full ahead together, keep both planes at hard-a-rise," Joe ordered briskly.

A trembling shook the boat as she answered to the surge of power. The depth held at two hundred and seventy feet — two hundred and seventy feet, yes, he could just hold her on the planes at this speed! But as the thunder of the attacking destroyers diminished, Joe was forced to reduce speed, and then the depth immediately began to swing away again — two hundred and eighty, ninety — Peter, sick in his stomach, could look no longer.

A violent shock rent the waters above them, a *crack!* that exploded in a savage roar of fury, to numb and daze the minds of the puny men in their steel coffin. The lights flickered and went out, as cork again showered down upon them from the deckhead.

Mercifully the emergency lamps flicked on to cast a pale light upon the pandemonium in the Control Room: men sprawled about the deck, now that the boat had taken up a steep bow-down angle. She was slipping fast now, sliding down to the hungry deeps, with three hundred feet on the gauge and the pointer hard up against the stops.

The phone shrilled from the after-ends.

"Water coming in through the stern glands, sir," Keating, the telephone operator reported, his young face sweating and deathly pale.

Joe clung to the ladder. *I dare not leave it any longer*, he thought, *it's now or never, and God help us if the airlines are fractured.* He turned towards Saunders, the imperturbable Outside E.R.A.

"Blow One Main Ballast!"

Saunders's hands were already poised over the panel. He leapt at the air valve and jerked it open.

Peter watched, fascinated. If the airline was fractured by the explosion, nothing could now save them from a hideous death, a horrible end that none of them had ever dared contemplate. He shut his eyes and prayed. He heard the air screaming along the thin pipe above his head. He waited to feel the lift of the deck beneath his feet, waiting during an eternity of time. Above the anguish of his consciousness the phone screamed. He opened his eyes to see Keating mouthing his report.

"Water out of control in the after-ends, sir."

"Stop blowing One Main Ballast. Blow Six Main Ballast!"

Saunders's hands snaked like lightning and the valves spun.

Then, later, aeons later, Peter found himself standing upright. Yes, the angle had come off and she was taking on a bow-up tilt! He swallowed and smiled at Joe when he felt the boat start to move upwards, even though the pointer was still against the stops, in spite of repeated tappings of the dial by the second coxswain.

"Stop blowing Six."

The screaming of the air ceased. They waited in an agonising silence. Was she really responding and coming up, or was she only momentarily lifting her bows while she still sank bodily?

A sigh rustled through the Control Room: the pointers on the gauge jerked away from the stops, two hundred and ninety, eighty — she was climbing away from the black depths, away, yes away — Peter could have screamed in exquisite relief!

Now she took on a steep bow-up angle and porpoised upwards. If she was out of the fresh water estuary, she would shoot out of the water, porpoising and out of control, she was so light.

Keating answered the phone. "Water stopped coming in, sir." The boyish face beamed.

"Very good," Joe replied tersely, for they were not out of the wood yet. He could not afford a break surface, and he would have to give away their position by releasing the air from the main ballast tanks.

"I'll have to risk it, Number One. Take over now, and catch a trim as quickly as you can."

Peter leapt to the gauges.

"Open main vents!" Joe ordered calmly, "port fifteen, steer o-two-o."

The boat was now leaping upwards alarmingly, but as soon as the vents were opened she immediately came under control at seventy feet. But the enormous air bubbles were frothing on the surface and the nearest hunter had already pounced upon them.

"Destroyer H.E. increasing, sir, right ahead."

"Very good. Midships, steady!"

"O-three-o, sir," the helmsman grunted.

"I'll go straight for her, Number One, and she should overshoot. Stand-by for an increase in speed!"

Already the fast-running engines reverberated overhead, thrashing towards them in an avalanche of sound.

"Five hundred yards, sir."

Joe waited, his iron nerve still intact. A split second out in his timing and he would drive the submarine into the centre of the exploding holocaust. Ian Taggart watched and waited breathlessly while the roar overhead overwhelmed them. Taggart forced back a yell of impatience, as still the Captain delayed.

"Group up, full ahead together!" Joe barked.

The phone buzzed, and seconds later, the longest seconds that Taggart had ever known, the boat trembled, shook herself and gathered speed.

As the thunder subsided overhead, they heard the click of the depth-charge primers. But *Rugged* was now moving fast, on opposite courses to her hunter. The submarine must at this very moment be immediately under the falling pattern.

"Hold your hats on!" Joe yelled in the uproar.

But the pattern exploded well astern of them, hardly jarring the boat.

"That fooled them!" Joe laughed, "now we'll give them the slip. Group down, slow ahead port, stop starboard. Steer o-six-o."

Peter sighed. They had had enough of this counter-attack. Slowly the Asdic impulses decreased and disappeared, as the confused hunters worried after their prey.

"H.E. fading, sir," Elliott reported unemotionally.

Joe grinned. "I'm fed up with this lark," he said. "Would anyone object if I shifted billet to another area?"

Peter smiled and a ripple of laughter ran through the Control Room.

"Open up from depth-charging, patrol routine."

The doors swung open and men smiled once more at each other. In the fore-ends, Bill Hawkins looked at Smith.

"What did I tell you, mate?" he said gruffly, "not so boring, was it?"

"Not 'arf, it weren't," Smith laughed, "but I wonder where the Old Man is taking us now?"

CHAPTER 4

Combined Effort

"Immediate signal, sir."

The Captain glanced up at the P.O. Tel. who stood by the Ward Room table, a pink slip of paper protruding from his outstretched hand. He held the pad steady while his Captain absorbed the contents.

Immediate. To Rugged *from Captain Tenth Submarine Flotilla. Shift patrol to position 180, Cape Rizzuto, 3 miles. Enemy convoy of four tankers, seven destroyers, course 220, speed 15 knots. Wellington torpedo-bombers will rendezvous at 2230 and will attack first. Time of Origin 0826.*

Joe grinned at Haig's face, tired and inscrutable with its lined pallor.

"Thank you, P.O. Tel. It's a long time since we had a decent target, isn't it?"

"Yes, sir, but we mustn't be greedy — we get our fair share of it," and he took his tired body aft to the tiny W/T office at the after end of the Control Room.

Joe paused thoughtfully before sending for Benson. Haig wasn't the only one who was showing signs of stress. They all badly needed sleep, and a break from these interminable weeks of strain. *But the job's got to be done*, Joe thought, *whether we like it or not*. He put down his book, stretched, and stifled a yawn which shook his relaxed frame. The glow from the few lights, the sudden warmth after the long night, and the contentment

43

which swept over him after one of O'Riley's breakfasts always made Joe feel drowsy. With an effort of will, he dragged himself into the Control Room, where for a moment he watched Taggart keeping his periscope watch. *He's coming on*, thought Joe — *he'll make a useful submariner one day.* Then the Captain moved over to the chart table where Benson, who had been laying off the course, made way for him.

"Where are we, Pilot?"

Benson pointed out the small mark of the pencil line on the chart.

"Here, sir."

Joe paused and, as he instinctively took the pair of dividers offered to him by the Navigating Officer, he expressed himself out loud.

"I suppose this is a reliable fix?"

"Yes, sir. Twenty minutes ago."

"Good … now how far off Cape Rizzuto are we?"

"Cape Rizzuto, sir? About thirty miles I think."

But Joe's mind had already begun to grapple with the problem, and once again he was soon his alert and cautious self, as he pricked the distances off on the chart.

"Yes. We'll get there on time, Sub, but we'll have to increase speed. It will be a night attack, so we ought to get in a bit of a charge first. Work out what speed I want to reach Cape Rizzuto by ten tonight."

Benson's eyes smiled.

"Aye, aye, sir. Something up?"

Joe fished the signal from his khaki shirt and opened it on the chart table.

"Sorry, Pilot, I'm slipping! I meant to show it to you. I'm going to get my head down."

"Aye, aye, sir."

By the time that Benson had adjusted *Rugged*'s course and speed, twenty minutes had passed. He went into the Ward Room to report to his Captain, but he had to shake him roughly to wake him.

"Course o-eight-seven, sir. Speed four knots."

Joe showed faint recognition before dropping back into a deep sleep.

"Very good, Pilot. Thank you."

Benson strolled back to the chart table for a last check. *Joe's as tired as all of us*, he thought, *he needs a rest*.

Rugged surfaced at eight-thirty, only twelve miles from the low-lying headland of Cape Rizzuto. Before the splashing water had drained from her casing, her signalman and Captain were clambering on to the bridge. A quick all-round look without binoculars, and Joe opened the voicepipe cock.

"Keep your eyes skinned, signalman. There's too much moon for my liking. There are bound to be aircraft about, searching ahead of the convoy."

"Aye, aye, sir." Goddard was sweeping the horizon through his binoculars, and to the north-eastward a smudge had already appeared in his field of view.

"Red six-o, sir. Land."

"Very good. That's Cape Rizzuto."

Joe crouched over the voicepipe.

"Start the generators. Stop the blowers. Lookouts on the bridge."

The First Lieutenant was still in the Control Room when he heard himself summoned to the voicepipe.

"Aye, aye, sir. I'll come up." He slipped his white submarine sweater over his head, and then scrambled up the conning tower ladder. Peter took a deep breath of the fresh air and allowed the goodness to find the furthest extremities of his lungs.

"Number One here, sir. What a grand night!"

The sea was dappled with dancing light, the reflection of the moon sparkling like myriads of diamonds.

"Grand night, my foot! It's a rotten night, a filthy, foul, beastly night, Number One. How the devil d'you think we can carry out a night attack on a night like this?"

Peter grinned foolishly to himself.

"And stop smiling, for Pete's sake, Number One. It's so light, I can even see your ugly mug grinning."

Already the moon was sinking in the western sky, so that the loom of the distant land seemed sombre and more defined. The two lookouts and Taggart, the Officer of the Watch, leant motionless against the bridge side as they strained through their binoculars.

Joe glanced at his watch and then spoke quietly to Peter.

"This is going to be a difficult attack, Number One. It's nine-fifteen so there's an hour to go before the Wimpeys arrive. I'll move out to the Eastward slightly so that I can put the convoy down-moon of us."

"The targets ought to stand out like houses on a night like this, sir," said Peter as he inhaled deeply in contentment.

"Blast you and your aesthetic appreciation, Number One. It's as clear as daylight for enemy aircraft, and we don't want to be put down by them or we shall miss the convoy."

Peter's eyes slid over the sleek fore-casing, now awash and sparkling with luminous phosphorescence.

"We ought to see them first, sir, trimmed down like this."

But Joe was watching Hawkins, the port lookout, who had his head cocked on one side.

"I thought I could hear aircraft, sir," Able Seaman Hawkins said from the port wings of the bridge.

The bridge personnel stiffened while five pairs of ears strained to hear the sickening throb. Then, slowly, gradually, there drifted upon their consciousness a low thrumming of engines.

"I'll get below, sir," Peter said quietly. He had already lowered himself over the lip of the conning tower hatch when he heard Taggart shouting.

"There, sir, Green six-o. Aircraft!"

"Clear the bridge! Dive, dive, dive!" and Joe spun round to press the klaxon push.

As Peter dropped on to the corticene of the Control Room below him, he felt the rungs of the ladder tremble from the vibration of the lookouts who were leaping down upon him. He heard the Captain yell, "First clip on!" and then he knew they were plunging downwards, eighteen — twenty — twenty-three feet. They were out of sight now and only the swirl of their screws would be showing.

Then Joe stood beside him, his Ursula suit crackling in the sudden silence.

"Blow Q."

Slowly the mad descent downwards lessened as the emergency tank was blown. Forty, forty-three, forty-six feet — and still no explosion from the bombing aircraft.

"Eighty feet."

"Eighty feet, sir."

"Lucky that time, Number One. If she had sighted us, the convoy would be alerted by now; then it would alter course, knowing that we lie across the line of advance."

"Yes, sir, assuming that no bomb means she hasn't sighted us."

Joe rubbed his chin, stubbly and shadowed with days of growth.

"I didn't think she was running in — she didn't seem to be diving on us."

"Well, sir, we'll soon know," Peter laughed. "It's ten o'clock now, and the convoy's due in half an hour."

"They've never been late yet!" and Joe chuckled to himself as he slung his binoculars round his neck. "But keep your fingers crossed about these aircraft. Lookouts in the tower, periscope depth."

And so, by twenty minutes past ten, *Rugged* lay trimmed down on the surface, only her conning tower and gun visible above the sparkling sea. She weaved slowly, four miles to the south-eastward of the low-lying Cape, invisible to all who were down-moon of her. But to those on the bridge, the waiting was exasperating.

"What's the time, Sub?" Joe snapped.

"Ten twenty-six, sir."

Joe grunted, and then he sighed as he looked at the darkening spur of headland, now black to the northward.

"There they go!" he whispered. "Group-up! Blow up all tubes!"

Taggart spun round. Then he saw a red flare tumbling from the blackness of the northern sky. Two miles, he judged it. The Captain was crouching over the compass, taking a bearing of the flickering flare.

"Bearing three-five-six — flares!" he yelled down the voicepipe. "Port ten, steer three four-o, full ahead together."

The little submarine shuddered to the full power as she surged ahead under her silent electric motors. Taggart swallowed while he strained his eyes through the binoculars.

Surely they must sight the enemy soon — the land was looming so close!

"That's more like it!" Joe chuckled and his arm stretched out right ahead. "There go the flares!" and he bent to take another bearing.

The flares seemed much closer now, great tumbling balls of white light, falling like thistledown from the lowering clouds.

"The Wimpeys will go in soon," Joe murmured, as he moved to the voicepipe. "Range three thousand yards, convoy and seven destroyers. Course two-two-o, speed fifteen knots. Stand-by all tubes, start the attack!"

He glanced up and as he did so a huge grin creased his face.

"Look, Sub! The Wimpeys have torpedoed tail-end Charlie!"

Taggart was feeling ashamed. He'd not sighted the enemy yet. How experience counted in these things, even to keeping a lookout! But there could be no doubt now. One of the dark silhouettes which slid across the field of his binoculars suddenly erupted into a ball of flame, and dark, oily smoke gushed out, streaming away into the distance as the convoy steamed onwards.

Joe took the binoculars from his eyes, for now the light of the setting moon threw the whole scene into broad relief, washing the sides of the white ships with a soft paleness. *Rugged* was up-moon and invisible, in a perfect attacking position.

But lunging upon her, so that she would be run down by them, came two weaving destroyers, wheeling angrily like excited wasps. One was already altering inwards and, as she turned, a gout of thick smoke spurted from her funnel. This streamed into a long plume which billowed outwards while she raced back to screen her protégés. The nearest destroyer was now less than a mile away, but, apart from weaving closely ahead of the port column, she maintained her mean line of advance. Then from her funnel also a black ribbon of smoke streamed to hide the convoy from view.

Joe's face was impassive at the turn of events. It was going to be a tricky attack, getting through that smoke. And the destroyer would be passing close to him — too close.

"Aircraft, red two-o!" Taggart shouted.

But Joe had already sighted it, and as the brute lumbered towards them he dived the boat.

"Clear the bridge!"

Peter heard the urgent command, even before the klaxon screamed. He took her down in less than nineteen seconds. The Captain scrambled out from the tower, and blurted breathlessly, "Starboard ten. Periscope depth."

"Blow Q," Peter ordered.

In the flurry, Peter stood quietly by the pump-order instrument, firmly in charge of the situation.

"More rise on the after-planes, Coxswain … take it off; that's better! Now, vent Q outboard."

The Outside E.R.A. flicked a lever on the panel, while with the other hand he operated the periscope lever.

"Twenty-three feet, sir," Peter reported, an amused smile on his face as he noticed the bewildered lookouts who still waited by the bulkhead door, tired of all this bobbing up and down.

"I'll stay here for a minute, Number One, as I can just see in the moonlight. I'll have to risk the aircraft," Joe said by the periscope.

"He probably didn't…" Peter started to reply, but a distant explosion rapped the pressure hull.

"I think he probably did, Number One!" Joe chuckled. "But he's a poor shot, and I hope it will keep him where we were." He paused, concentrating on a fixed bearing.

"Bearing THAT!"

"Red four-o, sir."

"Destroyer laying smokescreen, speed thirty knots, weaving on port bow of convoy. Range THAT; down periscope."

Benson calculated the range.

"Twelve hundred yards, sir."

"Course for a sixty track, Sub!" Joe snapped.

Taggart twiddled the knobs on his Fruit Machine.

"Two four-o, sir."

Joe was gazing intently at the depth gauges, his mind racing. Peter searched his face, and for a moment or two their eyes met. He did not like what he saw.

"I'm going to surface, Number One, as soon as this blighter slides past. He's on the port bow of the column, so if I can get through his smoke quickly, there ought to be time to get in a salvo." He spoke quietly and Peter sensed the desperate odds of the attack. The enemy was angry and fully alerted, first by the attacking Wellington torpedo-bombers, then by their own reconnaissance aircraft. The Italians knew what to expect, for this was not the first time submarine and torpedo-bomber had co-operated.

Elliott, the Asdic operator, looked up from his set, a pained expression on his deadpan face.

"There's H.E. all round, sir, but concentrated between red four-o and right ahead."

Even as Joe seized the periscope, he smiled.

"Very good — but keep on listening. Officer of the Watch and signalman in the tower. Stand by to surface!"

As Taggart clambered up to the upper hatch he could feel the thrum of fast-revving propellers dinning against his ears. He was breathless with excitement as he grasped the shorter of the two brass clips. He wrenched, and the clip came free.

"One clip off!"

His hands grasped the longer handle and he waited.

An uncontrolled terror froze his movements while the impact of his predicament struck him. Barely fifteen feet below the surface, he straddled upon an oily ladder, embraced in the blackness by the circular conning tower. He was thankful for the darkness in this agony of waiting, with the threshing of advancing propellers growing louder on his eardrums at every second. He tried to blot out his imagination but, straining his back against the conning tower, he felt creeping over him an insane desire to scream. *I can't stay here*, he thought. *I can't; but then, what will the others think, the Captain, Number One and the troops?* His hand clenched the rung of the ladder more firmly in the blackness, while all around him the water gurgled and the clamour pounded.

"Surface!"

From below there floated up to him the hoarse cry of the Captain, and then, before he had time to think, a whistle blew.

"A-ah!" Taggart sighed. "This is it."

He leant back and savagely wrenched at the remaining clip. The hatch sprang open over his head and water drenched him as the pale moonlight brought sanity flooding into his mind. Now, with action spurring him, his muscles reacted instinctively. He clambered out and jumped for the voicepipe cock. Suddenly he found himself upright, and as he looked over the side he began to choke.

The Captain reached the bridge side twelve seconds later and in a flash his mind took in the scene, a picture that was to be impressed on his mind for the rest of his life. In his heart, Joe Croxton had been dreading this attack. He had had too long waiting for it and his stomach had turned to water. The whole thing was so cold-blooded, so predetermined, that he had been forced to work out each move in his mind with precision. On his last periscope look he had judged that this was the correct moment to surface, and he was pleased to see that his old skill was improving and not deteriorating — after fourteen patrols the pundits said that one started to lose judgment, didn't they? All this flashed through Joe's mind when he reached the side, pleased by his correct appreciation of the developing attack.

Rugged was well up-moon. Swinging away from her like a wide pencil, the path of the moon's reflection pointed towards the darkening foreshore. Across this path of liquid moonlight the whole convoy now moved.

Well out on *Rugged*'s port bow, the first destroyer was disappearing behind the thick pall of smoke which was now billowing from her funnel. Joe could just see her wash boiling white before she disappeared into the black lane of smoke. *Rugged* would be plunging into this thick ribbon in less than five seconds, for already Joe's nostrils could smell the bitterness of the oil fuel in the curling smokescreen.

As *Rugged* started to enter the smoke, Joe caught sight of the advancing destroyer broad on his starboard bow. She was just outside the lane of billowing smoke which streamed from the leading destroyer, so that Joe caught sight of the bows which plunged deep into the water to send silver spray flying into the darkness. From her funnel too, gouts of curling smoke now poured as her screen spread across the water. At that instant, she must have sighted *Rugged* darting into the blackness, for, before the destroyer disappeared from sight, Joe glimpsed three white steam puffs, jerking from her sirens.

"Blast! She's sighted us!" Joe shouted above the whistling of the wind. "Lookouts clear the bridge! Stand by all tubes! Sub, come to the voicepipe and relay my orders."

Taggart scrambled around the compass to the voicepipe and then suddenly *Rugged* found herself in the swirling smoke.

Joe ducked underneath the lip of the bridge and took a deep breath. Around them swirled a writhing mass of half-burnt fuel, thick gobs of choking fumes, swinging and curling downwind. "Can't see in this," Joe cursed. "I might as well cross my fingers and wait for the crash."

Rugged was totally blind now, she knew not what lay on the other side of the smoke. Less than nine hundred yards away, a destroyer was searching for her and must now be cutting through the smoke to ram the submarine when she emerged from the enveloping screen. As *Rugged* plunged onwards, Joe and Taggart crouched, gasping on the bridge, eyes streaming and blind with tears from the acrid smoke.

"All tubes ready, sir!"

Joe heard the report, and his mind forced itself to think of the crisis about to face him in the next few seconds. Either *Rugged* would collide into an advancing tanker or she would be in a good firing position for a quick shot, providing the attacking destroyers gave her a chance.

Then suddenly, above the dark periscope standards which swayed above his head, a sheet of whiteness streamed by and he knew that they were leaving the smoke. He straightened up and felt his stomach heaving with nausea. But then the curtain of smoke drifted apart as *Rugged* swept out of the screen into the pale moonlight.

For a split second Joe took in the extraordinary scene, a tableau fixed in time. The whole incident seemed unreal, like toys on a nursery table, model ships on a plywood sea. Nothing moved, photographic in its immobility. Then the whole panorama came to life when the destroyer on the starboard quarter flashed out of the smoke. Swiftly she slid across the sparkling sea, heeling outboard as she put her wheel hard over to alter on to a ramming course. *She's less than five hundred yards now*, thought Joe, *but I've just got time…*

"Starboard twenty — steer o-six-five," he shouted as he crouched over the port torpedo sight. *Rugged* started to swing and the targets began to slide across the firing bar.

"Stand by!"

"Stand by!" Taggart yelled down the voicepipe.

The nearest ship was less than two hundred yards away. A great wall of metal she was, huge, white and gleaming in the moonlight. A heap of water piled up ahead of her blunt bows, and, out on her quarter, her wake curled and broke in sparkling phosphorescence.

Then Joe sighted her opposite number in the far column — a huge ship, well laden, with smoke pouring from her two funnels. *If I miss this nearer one, I can't fail to hit the further ship,* Joe's mind raced. *I'll fire a fraction early and try to hit both.*

"They're opening fire, sir!" Taggart yelled above the whining of the wind. An orange flash spurted on the fo'c'sle of the destroyer which now seemed terrifyingly close.

"Steady!" Joe ordered quietly.

"Steady, sir!" Taggart shouted down to the Control Room.

There was a spurt of flame, a bright flash, and a loud explosion well over on their port bow cracked their eardrums.

"Fire one!"

Taggart nearly missed the order, so calmly was it given in this split second of crisis. He was fascinated by the vee shape of the bows which scythed their way so certainly towards them. *Oh God!* thought Taggart, *this is the end — Joe is going to sink his ship but the destroyer will rip us open.* He could see the excited figures of sailors on the fo'c'sle of the destroyer.

"Fire by time interval! Dive, dive, dive!"

As Taggart repeated the order he lunged at the klaxon push, then leapt for the hatch. Before he fell into the blackness of the conning tower, he dimly registered the slight shudder of the torpedoes leaving their tubes. Joe stood waiting for him like a gentleman's gentleman, but before he jumped into the abyss of the conning tower his mind photographed the impending disaster.

The target ship had no time to avoid her fate, the first torpedo striking her amidships. Joe felt the scorching heat as the tanker exploded in a sheet of white and green flame, a horrible and unforgettable sight. Flaming petrol showered into the night, and the flames spread like quicksilver across the water, missing the threshing destroyer by a few feet.

"Hard-a-port!"

As Joe shut the hatch he caught a last glimpse of his potential avenger. A great bow reared above him, the white bone in her teeth gleaming in the moonlight. Over the guard rails a group of seamen hung, pointing excitedly. She was too close to use her gun now, and the weapon pointed drunkenly over the side. She was heeling hard over in a tight turn, trying to decrease her turning circle, for *Rugged* was turning inside her. Joe saw her cross-trees stark against the cirrus shining so whitely in the moonlit heavens. Then the hatch banged shut over him.

CHAPTER 5

"Game, Set, and Match"

"One clip on — eighty feet, shut off from depth-charging! Emergency astern together!"

From the darkness of the upper conning tower Peter heard the familiar voice, but this time there was a note of desperate urgency. Peter had nearly been overbalanced by the force of an explosion which had shaken the whole boat — the first torpedo hit, he hoped.

Then, as Taggart stumbled from out of the canvas trunking, Peter heard the mounting roar of the approaching turbines, the propellers singing and clattering in a cacophony of water noises. Peter gasped when he saw Taggart's ashen face.

The unusual order crackled from the tower, and then Joe was with them, his eyes flashing around the Control Room.

Even as the telegraphs clanged, Joe knew they had little chance. *Rugged* was to be ripped open within the next ten seconds, and the deep would swallow them. Ah well! *Rugged* had taken a tanker with her anyway... Then suddenly, above the pounding of the destroyer now scything towards them, another explosion shook the boat.

"That'll be another tanker!" Joe mused. He smiled wanly as a great cheer echoed from one end of the boat to the other. *What's the use?* he thought, *the poor chaps won't have much to shout about in a second or...*

"Shall I blow Q, sir?" Peter asked quietly.

"Not till I say so."

"Aye, aye, sir."

Thirty-two — thirty-four feet — no collision yet! *Rugged* was still grouped up and she must now be almost stopped in her tracks, the way entirely off her after the emergency astern; but she was sinking bodily, thanks to 'Q' which made her ten tons heavier.

Joe had taken the only possible action to avert disaster. Experience was his tutor, for by stopping the submarine he hoped that the destroyer would overshoot and pass over his fore-casing instead of his stern or conning tower.

Now he waited in his loneliness, no one, except perhaps Ian Taggart, guessing the dire secret that was locked in his heart. The destroyer was churning overhead at this very moment, and from beneath his lowered lids, Joe watched the upturned faces around him, the whites of their eyes gleaming. Joe wanted to shout, to laugh out loud at the comic faces peering upwards at the deckhead less than twenty-four inches above them. He felt his hands clasping and unclasping as his nerves fought for control.

If Flint makes a mistake over his switchboard drill when going full astern, thought Joe, *we're scuppered! Once again, the quality of the training I've tried to give 'em will mean life or death … if Flint blows those main fuses now…!*

The holocaust of sound which rumbled all around them centred over the fore-ends, hung, then swept quickly down the starboard side.

Joe passed a hand over his face and started to unfasten his Ursula suit. He unlooped his binoculars while Saunders, the Outside E.R.A., helped him out of his jacket.

"Phew!" Joe sighed. "I don't want any more of that."

"Midships, steer three-five-o."

"Fifty feet, sir," Peter reported quietly.

"Blow Q," the Captain ordered.

"Course three-five-o, sir," the helmsman murmured from the wheel.

Joe glanced at the Fruit Machine.

"I'm afraid we shall be passing right under our torpedoed target, Number One — o-ho! There go the charges!"

The destroyer's depth charges clanged harshly against the boat.

"Fooled them that time, sir!" Peter grinned.

Joe nodded. He was worried by the thought of what lay above them.

"Set all-round listening watch."

"Aye, aye, sir."

Elliott slid the earphones over his head, but lifted them momentarily while another pattern exploded harmlessly on their starboard quarter.

"If we can slip under our sinking ship," Joe murmured to Peter, "I think we shall throw them off when we get on to the far side of the convoy."

"Hope so, sir. They aren't expecting that."

"Breaking-up noises all round, sir," Elliott's voice broke in upon their conversation.

Joe grinned.

"Good-o! Can you give me a bearing?"

"All round, sir."

"Thought so — we've dodged the heat but risk being sunk by our own target!"

But Joe was not smiling. He leant against the ladder and watched Peter dealing with the trim. Curious cracklings and whistlings broke the silence in the waiting submarine: the bulkheads of the sinking ship were going.

The trouble lies in my imagination, Peter thought. *I used to be all right, but now everything is too vivid.* He fixed his eyes on the depth gauge and concentrated. *Rugged* must be directly under the sinking ship by now, and even without the Asdics they could hear the ship breaking up above them.

The silence in the Control Room was electric. Each man was waiting for the sickening lurch and the jolt that meant they were pinned beneath the spiralling wreckage.

"We're nearly..." the Captain began.

He was looking at Peter, but he halted his sentence midway when he saw his First Lieutenant's face. Peter had gone white. Then from for'd Joe heard a tearing noise, like tinplate being ripped. Men held their breath, while Peter spun round to watch his gauges.

An almost imperceptible bow-down angle was slowly apparent and Peter had to compensate by pumping out from for'd. Then a gentle slapping tapped against the side, regularly, maddeningly, the echoes reverberating through the boat.

"This will whistle up all the destroyers for miles around, Number One."

"Reckon something's across our jumping-wire, sir, and flapping on to the fore-casing."

Joe jumped for the chart.

"What have we got under us, Pilot?"

"Twelve fathoms, sir."

"That's fine! They'll think this din is our target breaking up. I'll go on for another two minutes and then bottom her. Start taking her down, Number One."

"Aye, aye, sir."

Rugged forged ahead slowly, the flapping on her casing growing fainter as she lost speed.

"One hundred and forty feet, sir."

"Stop both."

The order was passed by word of mouth and, as the way came off her, the clattering on the casing ceased. There was a gentle scraping as she touched bottom, she took on a slight list to port, and then all was still.

A sigh floated through the boat, and then you could feel the tensions relax: men started to whisper and smile again.

"Carry on with your all-round sweep, please, Leading Seaman Elliott. Report when they've all passed over. I'm going to get my head down."

Elliott smiled. "Aye, aye, sir," he said, and he bent once more over his set.

Peter looked at the clock and could hardly believe his eyes — eleven forty-five — only a quarter of an hour before midnight! Surely it must be later than that? He felt that he'd passed through a lifetime since ten-fifteen. He handed the watch over to Benson and then slumped on to the nearest settee in the Ward Room.

He passed his fingers through his ruffled hair and gazed with admiration at the exhausted figure that lay stretched out horizontally on the opposite settee. Joe was asleep already, his breathing coming regularly and deeply.

"He knows how to relax," Peter whispered to himself. "If ever I am given a boat I must try to remember his secret. He must be absolutely whacked!"

Peter climbed over the table and crawled into his bunk. The rough blankets comforted him as he rolled himself contentedly into them. For a few moments he let his mind travel over the miracle of the events of the night, and then once again he became aware of the merciful guidance of the good God who had protected them. With a sigh of gratitude and relief he slipped into unconsciousness.

"Diving stations in five minutes' time."

Peter slowly dragged himself from his bunk. The clock showed one-fifteen in the morning and when they surfaced it would be his watch on the bridge. In a dream he pulled on his thick sweater, found his binoculars and clambered into his Ursula suit. He went to the gauges and waited for orders, still half asleep.

"All-round sweep completed, sir. Nothing to report."

"Periscope depth."

Peter slowly took her up and five minutes later they were wallowing on the surface.

"Permission for the First Lieutenant on the bridge?"

"Permission granted."

When Peter reached the bridge, the second Coxswain had already cleared the wreckage that had dangled from the jumping wire. *Rugged* was going astern and the twisted girder that had caused the tell-tale noise was being plumped over the bows.

"Thank heavens that's gone, Number One. It's been a busy night, hasn't it?"

"Yes, sir. But worth it — you sank two ships."

Joe paused.

"We, you mean, Number One."

"Yes, sir."

There was a long pause while the two men sucked in deep draughts of fresh air, so clean and fresh after the long hours below.

"We'll get in a good charge now anyway, Number One. We may need it tomorrow."

"Where are we off to now, sir?"

"The Iron Ring."

"Taranto — the naval base?"

"That's right," Joe replied.

Peter was silent for a moment.

"The best defended port on the south coast?" he asked.

"That's right, Number One."

From aft the drumming of the generators pounded in their ears, but Peter was silent. Taranto — the very name was dreaded.

CHAPTER 6

Ocean Pirate

"I don't like this visibility."

Hanging from the periscope handles, Joe Croxton peered intently into the haze.

"Down periscope," he continued. "I can't give you a fix, Pilot. There's nothing to see."

Rugged had been ordered to take up the end position on the left of the Iron Ring off Taranto. They had been unable to fix their position during the night and were hoping to take bearings at daylight, but now this fog had descended and they were lost.

"Any sign of our other boats, Elliott?" the Captain asked, but the H.S.D. could hear nothing on his Asdic set.

Joe scratched his head and went to the chart table where Benson was slumped hopelessly: a small dot on the chart represented his estimated position and that put *Rugged* ten miles south of Taranto.

Sub-Lieutenant Taggart was keeping his periscope watch, Peter Sinclair had turned in for his morning's sleep, and it was eleven o'clock before Taggart reported that the sun was beginning to break through the haze.

"Diving stations!" the Captain ordered.

Peter scrambled from his bunk, and dragged himself to his position between the depth gauges, expecting another attack, but to his relief Joe was smiling.

"I'm only bobbing up for a snap sun-sight, Number One. I'll have to be quick for we aren't far off the enemy beach," he said as he stood poised by the ladder, sextant in hand.

"Surface!"

Peter surfaced the boat, Taggart keeping an all-round lookout with the periscope, whilst the Captain climbed through the conning tower, followed swiftly by Benson with the deck-watch. With the sun balefully breaking through the haze, there was just enough visibility to see the horizon. In less than a minute, Joe had taken his sight, but there was no need to work it out.

"Look, sir!" Benson expostulated, his arm outstretched.

Joe spun round.

Less than a quarter of a mile away and glistening in the weak sunlight, there broke through the fog for an instant the faint but unmistakable outline of Taranto breakwater.

"Good heavens!" Joe shouted. "Dive! Dive! Dive!"

They regained periscope depth and then Joe spoke his thoughts aloud.

"I don't think," he said to Peter, "that we were sighted. But I've got a position now and that puts us a quarter of a mile from the breakwater and slap in the middle of the enemy minefield."

"That's nothing new, sir," Peter grinned. "Couldn't be worse than our last Piccadilly trip, could it?"

There was a rumble of laughter through the Control Room. The unforgettable memory of the rasping mine wire was hardly nostalgic.

But it was a tense two hours nevertheless. It was unpleasant steering a course through the mines which grew as thick as a forest, swaying on their steel-wire stalks from the seabed. Neither was it a pleasant sensation to know that they might collide with their friends who were forming an Iron Ring around Taranto. But by four o'clock they were in position at the western extremity of the Ring, three miles from the coast and five miles from the next boat — Harry Arkwright in *Restless*. At seven p.m., Peter was about to hand over the periscope to Benson.

"Visibility is still poor, Pilot. The land to the westward is fading now."

Peter swung the periscope towards the land.

"Bearing is THAT."

"Red five-o, sir."

"That's the last we shall see of Italy tonight," Peter said to Benson, "I'll just…"

As he started his last all-round sweep he halted.

"Captain in the Control Room!" he shouted.

There was a clatter from the Ward Room and then Joe streaked into the Control Room.

"What is it, Number One?"

"U-boat, sir, bearing Red two-o."

Holding the periscope steady, Peter put the Captain on the bearing.

"Diving stations! Start the attack, target U-boat, bearing THAT!"

Joe's orders crackled through the boat like a bush fire.

"Red one-five, sir."

"I'm ten degrees on his starboard bow. Range THAT!"

The shining tube sped downwards as men silently bustled to their stations.

"Range nine hundred yards, sir," Benson reported from the chart table.

"Course for a sixty track?"

Ian Taggart adjusted the box of tricks called the Fruit Machine.

"O-two-five, sir."

"Up periscope. Stand by all tubes, starboard ten, steer o-two-five."

Peter was wrestling with his trim. There was a glassy calm on the surface and little periscope must show if it was not to be sighted. The movement of the hands as they scrambled aft always upset the trim to give the boat a bow-up angle and Peter was desperately transferring water from the after trimming tank to for'd.

In two strides Joe transferred to the attack periscope; he snapped his fingers and it slid upwards with a hiss.

"Twenty-two feet, sir," Peter reported, "twenty-one feet."

Swiftly Joe spun round on the after periscope. No aircraft! He was bent almost double now, trying to show as little of the periscope as possible.

"Twenty-feet, sir!" Peter reluctantly reported.

"For Pete's sake don't break surface and don't speed up or she'll see us. Use Q if you have to," Joe snapped. "Bearing THAT, range THAT, and I'm fifty degrees on her starboard bow!"

"Red five, sir."

"Six hundred yards, sir," Benson chanted.

Feverishly Taggart fed the information into the Fruit Machine, whilst above him the 'torpedo-ready' lamps flickered on one by one.

"Course for a sixty track, sir, o-three-o, D.A., red one-two, all tubes ready!"

"Nineteen feet, sir," Peter shouted, with only another foot to go before breaking surface, "flood Q!"

The Captain was slithering around the corticene on his stomach.

"Put me on my D.A.," he ordered crisply. "Down periscope, stand by all tubes!"

In the tension, no one even noticed the roar of Q tank as the foul air was vented inboard.

With a sigh, Peter watched the depth hover at nineteen feet, then the extra weight took control.

"Twenty-one feet, sir!" he breathed with relief.

The Outside E.R.A. held the periscope on the bearing, as the thin tube slid upwards once more.

"Stand by!" Joe yelled, "down periscope!"

"Stand by!" Taggart passed down the telephone to the tube-space.

The tension in the boat was unbearable: the hated U-boat was the finest target of them all.

Joe snapped his fingers and uncoiled himself from the deck when the attack periscope flashed by. All faces watched the tensed figure, the very personification of pent-up concentration, as a thin pencil of daylight streamed into the eye which peered so intently through the eyepiece.

Joe was elated. He was in a perfect firing position and he could plainly see the men on the bridge of the U-boat only a few hundred yards away. They were bare-chested and were evidently enjoying the hot sun as it filtered through the haze. The light grey U-boat stood up like a house, she was so close, her engine exhausts wisping at her stern and a white flurry foaming at her shark-like bows.

Joe couldn't believe his eyes. As the target started to slide across the cross-wire of the periscope, white foam spouted upwards from the U-boat and the grey image disappeared.

"She's dived!" Joe groaned, and a moan of frustration whispered through the boat.

Peter wiped his hands across his shorts. He was sweating in the excitement and heat, beads of perspiration trickling from his forehead. Joe grinned at him sardonically.

"We'll never get a chance like that again, Number One," Joe said. "I must have been showing too much stick and he sighted it."

"My fault, sir," Peter replied regretfully. "I nearly broke surface."

"Can't be helped," Joe snapped, "but I wonder what he'll do now. Up periscope."

The swirl still remained on the surface, and a trail of disappearing bubbles marked where she had been seconds ago. It was a tantalising reminder.

Then in the evening light, two hundred yards away, a grey tube sliced the mirror-like surface, to leave a tell-tale slick bubbling behind it.

"Bearing, THAT!" Joe snapped, "it's her periscope! Eighty feet!"

CHAPTER 7

Blind-Man's-Buff

"Silent routine!"

The silence in *Rugged* was complete. A grim game of cat and mouse was being played out, and one of the two submerged submarines would soon be lying at the bottom of the Mediterranean, twisted and burst asunder. The U-boat had turned the tables on them with a vengeance. Joe had allowed her to take the initiative, for he had already experienced this form of underwater attack between two submarines, when he had been First Lieutenant of a submarine in the Baltic. He was in no hurry.

"I'll stay at eighty feet and let him bat first," he told the Control Room. "Pass the word what I am doing and stand by all tubes for a snap attack. Again, I repeat there must be absolute silence — a carelessly dropped spanner may be the end of us."

So in the blackness of the deeps the two opposing submarines stalked each other. The U-boat stayed at periscope depth, trying to catch sight of her opponent, but *Rugged* had slid gently down to eighty feet. Joe refused to be hustled and would not expose his position by transmitting on his Asdics or by increasing speed.

"Well, Elliott, it's up to you! You are our eyes, ears and even nose — try smelling him out!"

Elliott's black head looked up from his Asdic set and his thoughtful eyes were smiling.

"All-round listening watch, please, Elliott."

"Aye, aye, sir."

Elliott bent himself to the work in hand, his keen ears tuned to pick up the slightest sound, and he could feel the eyes of all in the Control Room boring into his back as he crouched over the dimly-lit dials in his corner.

The U-boat also refused to transmit, so it was a weird and horrible game. The result depended upon who had the strongest nerves, and, watching Joe Croxton at this moment, everyone had confidence. But presumably the German submarine commanding officers had their Croxtons too? It was uncanny to feel that within two hundred yards of *Rugged* their slippery enemy prowled. Supposing there was an underwater collision? Peter closed his eyes momentarily to shut out the hideous picture.

"Slow H.E., green three-o, sir."

"Starboard five — I won't let her get away," Joe murmured and *Rugged* slowly swung to the bearing so that she was end-on to the U-boat. An audible sigh of relief could be felt when *Rugged* presented her minimum target.

"H.E. growing louder, sir. Very faint water noises. I should say she is travelling on 'slow-one'."

"Thank you, Elliott," Joe acknowledged calmly. "In that case she must be able to hear us too. I daren't stop both, Number One, for you'd have to pump, wouldn't you?"

"Yes, sir, I'm afraid so."

"I think she's still at periscope depth and that she reckons we're there too. He must be getting fed up looking for our periscope!"

Waiting for the U-boat to fire required iron nerves, and in the silence the tension was electric. But as Joe stopped speaking, a dull thud shook the boat.

"Torpedo fired, sir," Elliott snapped, for the first time a note of excitement in his report.

Peter held his breath whilst the lethal weapon spurted towards them. It was uncanny to feel that somewhere above them a ton of destruction hurtled remorselessly, intent on searching them out. There immediately followed a growing crescendo of noise, whistling and roaring down upon them. Swiftly there followed five more thuds, and the noise became a cacophony of sound. Now the torpedoes must strike, now, now…

Then the thrashing overwhelmed them. The clatter drew overhead and then slowly decreased into the distance.

"Six, wasn't it, Elliott?"

"Yes, sir, definitely six torpedoes."

"That's good — it must be his full outfit. What's his bearing now?"

"Drawing quickly down the starboard side, sir. She's very close."

In the silence a faint kerfuffle of water noises could just be heard whispering overhead.

"Very good, starboard ten," Joe beamed, "now it's our turn. He's fired all his torpedoes and we can stalk him at our leisure."

Men relaxed from their unnaturally stiff postures, as they realised that the boot was now on the other foot.

"Just in case he has another torpedo standing by, Number One, I shall fire from deep. Set all torpedoes to run at twenty-five feet."

"Aye, aye, sir." Taggart passed the order, and the mauve 'torpedo-ready' lamps flickered on and off while the adjustments were made.

"All torpedoes ready, sir."

The hunt could now begin, and the torpedoes would lunge up from eighty feet to the set depth. Joe was going to make no mistake and was taking his time.

"Start transmitting on Asdic."

Elliott was now in his element, for upon him depended success or failure. His steady hand tapped out the searching impulses and it was not long before he was in contact.

"In contact, sir, green two-o."

"Very good. We've almost gone full circle! Any idea of range?"

"About eight hundred yards, sir." Elliott reported after a pause.

"Bearing?"

"Steady, sir."

"What's his course, Sub?"

"O-four-o, sir. You are one hundred and twenty degrees on his starboard bow."

"Good, that's excellent. Speed, Elliott?"

"About four knots, I should say, sir."

"All right. What's my D.A.?"

"Red four, sir."

"Stand by all tubes!"

"Stand by, sir."

"Fire when I swing past her — starboard five."

"Starboard five, sir," the helmsman grunted, a note of intense excitement in his gruff voice.

"Three degrees to go, sir."

"Range eight hundred yards, sir, bearing steady."

"Two degrees to go, sir!"

Joe stood legs astride, watching the compass, his eyes flickering.

"Stand by all tubes!"

CHAPTER 8

U-93

"*Gott in Himmel!*" Ober-Leutnant Brandt exploded. "We missed!"

Three long minutes had dragged by, but still there were no explosions as the diminishing sound of their six torpedoes faded distantly.

Brandt rounded on his hydrophone operator.

"You must have been out with your bearings, you fool!"

But the operator remained mute — Brandt's temper was vicious.

"Up periscope!"

Brandt swung round the glassy surface, but then he impatiently banged shut the periscope handles.

"Can't see the English swine, curse him. Lucky I kept my stern tube, though, wasn't it, *Herr Leutnant?*" he snarled at his second-in-command, as he unconsciously sought justification from his subordinate. For he was a U-boat Captain of the second rank: Doenitz had sent his best men to the Atlantic. Brandt knew this, but his pride did not relish being classed as second-rate, and he hated operating in the Mediterranean, with its restricted waters.

Now Brandt was nervous. He dared not increase speed for fear of giving away his position. He knew the Englishman was within a few hundred yards of him and in his bones he felt that he was being stalked. But why had he not sighted the enemy periscope?

"Up periscope," he snapped.

"*Achtung, mien Kapitan!*" The yellow face of the hydrophone operator mouthed apprehensively.

Brandt's fingers tightened on the periscope handles, for he had heard it too. He remained peering through the eyepieces for he did not want to show the fear staring from his eyes.

Tick-tick, tick-tick-tick…

The grey faces in the Control Room of the U-boat glanced grotesquely across at one another. The U-boat was powerless now, except for one torpedo in the stern tube — only a snap shot with that could save them, and their ineffective Kapitan could not even see their hunter.

"Down periscope!"

Tick-tick, tick-tick-tick… Faster now, the impulses were beginning to swamp them.

Like a cornered rat, Brandt's wild eyes darted about the Control Room.

"Fool, what bearing?" he demanded of his hydrophone operator, and he strode across to the unfortunate man and shook him roughly by the shoulder.

A startled face jerked upwards.

"*Mein Kapitan*, I cannot tell. The impulses are all around and I cannot hear his propellers!"

There was no need for him to state the obvious. The frequency of the transmissions had increased rapidly, and they could now be heard by all in the U-boat: the morale of U-93 was bad and the ship's company were jumpy. Men were snarling angrily in the dark corners and casting accusing glances at Brandt. He had let them down and now they were to pay the price for his incompetence.

A senior rating stepped forward in the agonising tension.

"*Mein Kapitan!*"

"*Ja?*"

"We're caught like rats in a trap — can't you hear the Englishmen?" Once more they listened to the steady impulses, much faster they came now, the immediate prelude to the unleashing of the deadly torpedoes.

Brandt grunted and looked away, his mind working feverishly for some way out.

Tick-tick, tick-tick, tick-tick... Rapidly now, in a continuous stream —

The older man who spoke for the crew could contain himself no longer. He was a veteran of the Wolf Packs and his nerves were taut.

"For the Führer's sake, *mein Kapitan*, blow tanks and escape on the surface!" he screamed shrilly. They had not a moment to lose.

A flash of enlightenment sparked in Brandt's eyes.

"Surface? Why yes, of course," he mumbled to himself. He wiped his sweating palms on his trousers and looked around. "You all witness this, men?" he shrilled. "I am being asked to surface by the crew. I am not running away, am I?" his mad eyes pleaded.

"For the Führer's sake, get on with it, *mein Kapitan*," the senior rating shouted, as he strode truculently towards Brandt. "We'll discuss legalities afterwards."

The crafty smile of madness creased Brandt's grey face.

"Surface!" he whispered.

In *Rugged*'s Control Room, Taggart crouched over the mouthpiece of the telephone, waiting for Joe's crisp order, "Fire one!" — and that should have been the prelude to the end of the U-boat.

"She's blowing tanks, sir!" Elliott's voice crackled in the silence.

"She's WHAT?" the Captain blurted out, as he spun round to face his H.S.D.

"Blowing tanks, sir," continued Elliott imperturbably.

"I'm certain of it, bearing right ahead."

Joe's response was instinctive.

"Periscope depth, quickly, Number One!"

Peter took her up in less than a minute, to settle nicely at twenty-eight feet.

"Up periscope … bearing THAT, I'm forty degrees on her port bow and she's coming straight towards us!"

Joe slammed the periscope handles shut. There was no time to lose.

"There's something odd going on, Number One, they look panicky. I think I'll try a fish just across her bows… I wonder?" and Joe scratched his head. "Stand by to fire one."

"Stand by to fire one, sir," Taggart repeated down the phone.

The periscope hissed upwards.

"Fire one!" Joe snapped, and then the boat shivered.

"Torpedo running, sir," Elliott reported.

Joe was glued to the periscope, watching every move. The trail of bubbles from the track of the torpedo passed fifty yards ahead of the U-boat.

Joe spluttered unintelligibly.

"Well, I'll be … they're abandoning ship, Number One, look," and he handed over the periscope to his First Lieutenant.

Peter could not believe his eyes. The U-boat was losing way and starting to circle in a wide arc. She came to a standstill, and, from her bridge and superstructure, along her fore-casing and from her gun sponson, figures ran wildly to hurl themselves into the placid sea.

"Look at her after periscope, sir," Peter exclaimed, and he handed back the periscope to the Captain.

Joe was grinning as he glanced up from the eyepieces.

"Well, chaps, there's a white flag flying from her after standard — this must be the first time a U-boat has surrendered to one of His Majesty's submarines. It must be because we've had so much of our periscope showing for so long. He reckons we've got him taped — and perhaps we have!"

Joe paused, scratched his head, and thought aloud as was his usual custom.

"I don't trust these Huns, Number One. I'll circle her just in case she's called up reinforcements, but, meanwhile, get a boarding party ready."

So for the next twenty minutes, while Peter organised six ratings and the second coxswain, Petty Officer Weston, and the L.T.O., Leading Seaman Flint, into a boarding party, *Rugged* circled the U-boat which wallowed gently in the glassy calm.

"What an incredible performance!" muttered Joe as he hung from the periscope handles. "All the crew are still bobbing about in the water and they seem fascinated by my periscope. Perhaps they are terrified of my firing another fish — the explosion of a torpedo a hundred yards away can't be good for one's insides, so they have an excuse for being windy! But what a performance all the same!"

Joe flicked the periscope to low power and swept the horizon.

"No aircraft, Number One, and I don't think this is a trap. Boarding party all ready?"

"Yes, sir, except for the officer — shall I send the Sub?"

"No, you ass! I want *you* to go and take her over. I'll pick up the U-boat's crew, except for a few key hands which you may keep to help you dive the boat. Then follow me straight back to Malta."

"Me, sir?" Peter was dumbfounded but elated. "Me? Aye, aye, sir!" and he leapt into the Ward Room to grab his cap, and to snatch a revolver from the locker. As he re-entered the Control Room, Goddard, the signalman, pushed a white bundle, slashed with scarlet, into his arms.

"You'll be needing this, sir?"

Peter looked at the White Ensign.

"Thank you, Goddard: *Rugged*'s first prize — I hope!" and he snapped the holster of the pistol around his middle.

Peter mustered his party and checked that they had their gear, which included a length of chain, toggle-fitted at one end to keep open the upper hatch of the U-boat. He handed this to Able Seaman Hawkins, the burly three-badgeman who had been with Peter on his last adventure.

"Boarding party ready, sir," Peter reported.

"Right. Do you understand your orders?" demanded the Captain.

"Absolutely, sir, except for one thing."

"And what's that?" Joe snapped.

"How do we get across to the U-boat?" grinned Peter.

"Swim, you idiot; all of you will swim and, once across, we'll transfer gear by heaving line. Is that all?" Joe was smiling too.

"Yes, sir."

Joe had another all-round sweep and then Peter surfaced the boat. It was strange to be wallowing on the surface and to know that in a few seconds he would no longer be First Lieutenant of *Rugged* — but instead temporary Captain of a U-boat.

"Boarding party on the bridge!"

Peter led his party swiftly up the conning tower ladder and down to the fore-casing, where they handed their revolvers and gear over to Able Seaman Stack.

The sunlight dazzled them after the artificial lighting down below, and in the beauty and warmth of the afternoon, the whole scene seemed unreal to Peter. *Rugged* lay pointing directly at U-93: one torpedo from *Rugged*'s tubes would be all that was necessary, but preferably not after the boarding party were on board.

Joe leant over the bridge.

"Go on, this isn't a Women's Institute meeting — get cracking!"

Barely twenty yards separated the two submarines when Peter ran for'd on the casing. He leapt into the water to clear the pressure hull and struck out for the U-boat. Dimly he remembered seeing the matted heads of Germans bobbing in the distance, and then he found his hands grasping the free-flood holes of the U-boat's casing. In no time he was aboard, his feet firmly planted on the enemy ship, and he leant down to heave the first member of the boarding party after him. While they mustered on deck a heaving line hissed through the air to plop at their feet; Hawkins grabbed it and rushed for the bridge where he belayed the line. It was hauled taut by *Rugged* and then a second line snaked across, *Rugged*'s end being secured to a bucket. By hauling in on the second line, Hawkins swung the bucket across on the improvised jackstay and, after three hauls, all the gear was transferred, pistols, flares, and the length of chain. Hawkins slipped the heaving lines and *Rugged* went astern slowly. Joe yelled at the swimming Germans and began plucking them from the water.

The whole operation took over half an hour, and during this long period they were not molested, even by an aircraft. Peter sighed with relief when he finally saw Joe wave from *Rugged*'s bridge. Then he watched her slide beneath the surface and he felt distinctly embarrassed when he saw *Rugged*'s periscope slowly circling about a cable clear. Peter waved at the blue periscope and then grappled with the task in hand.

By now the boarding party had taken over down below, the chain and toggle firmly inserted in the upper lid by Hawkins — in case of treachery. The party had been strengthened by Sub-Lieutenant Taggart and another six hands from *Rugged*. In addition, the German engineer, electrician and coxswain had been taken aboard U-93, and these were now surlily showing the Englishmen how to dive the boat.

At last Peter was satisfied, and, with his heart in his mouth, he pulled the upper hatch shut over his head. He climbed down the conning tower ladder to the waiting Control Room below.

The faint whine of electric motors was the only sound to be heard. Able Seaman Bill Hawkins lounged in the for'd corner of the Control Room, pistol cocked and pointed at the German engineer who leant insolently against the complicated panel. Petty Officer Weston, the second coxswain, was on the after planes, Able Seaman Bowles on the fore planes, and they both looked up at Peter and grinned. Weston jerked his head towards the German engineer.

"Fritz can speak English, sir, but he's not over enthusiastic! He wants watching, I reckon."

Peter turned towards the German.

"Listen, Fritz. Listen carefully, if you know what's good for you," he said as he stared the German in the eyes. "If you don't obey orders instantly and co-operate, Able Seaman Hawkins here will shoot you out of hand. Any funny business and you're a dead duck. Understand?"

Bill Hawkins grinned in the corner. The German continued to lounge against the panel and he spat derisively on the deck.

"*Ja*, I understand, but I'll take you all with me, *mein Leutnant*," and he spat again, a sneer on his sallow face.

With one bound, Hawkins was alongside him, his face grim and his hands trembling with rage. He braced his huge shoulders and a thick arm shot out to pick up the German like a kitten by the scruff of the neck. Shaking the German until the teeth rattled in his head, Hawkins glared at him, saying with deceptive quietness, "Heinie, show some respect to our officer or I'll pulverise you."

Ian Taggart was on the periscope while this drama was being played out, and now his voice cut in upon the scene.

"Number One, sir — I mean Captain, sir — all-round sweep completed: nothing in sight."

Peter went up to the German, his eyes boring into him.

"Dive the boat," he ordered quietly.

CHAPTER 9

A Desperate Throw

For a second the engineer hesitated, but a savage jab of Hawkins' pistol made him jump with pain. He sprang to attention automatically.

"*Ja, mein Kapitan*," and with a sly smile his hands snatched at the main vent levers on the panel.

"That's better, Fritz," prompted Bill Hawkins. "Keep remembering your manners, that's all."

Peter snatched the periscope from Taggart.

"Sub, work the periscope lever and when the boat is down give me a course for Malta."

"Aye, aye, sir."

"Hard-a-dive on both planes, and speed up on the main motors: we'd better get a move on. Hawkins, watch Fritz!"

"Aye, aye, sir, I will that," a deep voice boomed from the panel.

The U-boat had now taken up a sharp bow-down angle and the gauges showed eight metres. Peter crouched at the periscope, and, as the lens dipped below the surface, he sighed audibly. It was good to leave that glassy calm, for it was miraculous that no patrolling aircraft had lumbered upon them. He left the periscope and, while Taggart went to the chart table whereon was still spread the current German chart, Peter took up his position between the two planesmen.

"Periscope depth is about ten metres, isn't it, Fritz?" Peter asked the German over his shoulder.

" *Ja.*"

"*Ja* — what?" growled Hawkins with another persuasive jab of the revolver.

The German grunted.

"*Ja, mein Kapitan.*"

"Ten metres then, Coxswain," Peter ordered.

"Ten metres, sir."

Peter soon had the boat trimmed. She seemed easier than *Rugged*, either because she was larger or because *Rugged*'s most skilled ratings were operating the valves and pumps.

Taggart looked up from the chart.

"Course for Malta, two-two-o, True, sir."

"Very good, Sub. Steer two-two-o."

The U-boat slowly swung to her new course.

"Well, here we go, men — next stop Malta!" Peter grinned. It was strange to have a command of his own, even though it was temporary and an enemy one at that. But Peter was under no illusions: two nights and all the day lay between them and the haven of Malta and much could happen in that time, particularly with his skeleton crew and this strange enemy submarine some of whose men were suicidal Germans.

After fixing their position and readjusting their course, Peter decided to go deep. At eighty feet they would be invisible from patrolling aircraft and could increase their speed, but the main danger would be from the few Germans whose attitude was unpredictable. If he could master the trimming and change of depth, the only other obstacle was the starting of the main engines for the battery charge when they surfaced at night.

Before going deep, Peter walked through the U-boat to familiarise himself with the different machinery, although all submarines were the same basically. He wanted to see for himself how the other Germans were getting on.

In the Engine Room, Stoker O'Connor greeted him with a grin. He was naked for he had spread his clothes over the engine's casing to dry.

"Excuse my rig, sorr, please, but I was a bit damp, if ye'll onderstand."

"That's all right, O'Connor. Have you got a hang of the machinery?"

"Sure, sorr! Putting on a charge will be as aisy as kiss your 'and. Leading Seaman Flint in the Motor Room there, and oi, have got it all worked out, sorr, sure we 'ave."

Peter grinned and passed through to the Motor Room where Flint stood over a fair-haired German of about twenty-three.

"Well, Flint, have you got your switchboard taped, because I want to carry out some drill?"

"Yes, sir. It's been much easier than I thought because this Hun is surprisingly helpful: he wants to get to Malta alive!"

Peter's face was grave.

"Wish I could say the same for the engineer, Flint. He's a crafty devil and I don't trust him: he doesn't seem to think there's much future for the crew of U-93 anyway. During the next half hour we're very much in his hands, as he is the only one who knows vents and airlines. So keep on your toes, Flint."

"Yes, sir, I will."

Peter strolled back to the Control Room, his heart thumping. Now for the crucial test: could he take her deep and get back again?

The tension in the Control Room was electric. The figures that waited were so motionless, they might have been marble statues. While Hawkins leant against the domed top of a spinning gyro, his eyes fixed on the German like a lynx, Fritz watched Peter's return from beneath half-closed eyes. Wheel spanner in hand, he sat on his haunches by the complicated panel and he did not rise at Peter's entry.

Peter deliberately walked past the man, went to the planesmen and turned about so that he was facing the panel and the German engineer.

To Peter, his own words sounded hollow above the gentle whine of the electric motors when he addressed the German.

"I am now going to drill the crew. You will work the panel."

The German nodded.

"*Ja, mein Kapitan.*"

"I am aware that you may try to sink the boat. I must warn you that the slightest indication of treachery will mean instant retaliation on our part. I mean to reach Malta and you are not going to stop us. Do you understand?"

Fritz's face was ashen.

"*Ja, mein Kapitan*, I understand."

"Able Seaman Hawkins," Peter continued.

"Sir?"

"Watch the engineer and the panel while I get on with the trimming."

"Aye, aye, sir," and a huge grin creased Hawkins' face.

Peter spoke quietly.

"Open all main vents."

The engineer turned his back on Peter and he faced the panel. His hands flickered over four small levers which were grouped closely together. The thudding of the vents clearly echoed through the boat.

"Check all main vents open," Peter ordered.

There was no sudden downward swoop, no change in depth, the pointers still showed ten metres.

"All main vents checked open, sir," Hawkins reported.

So far so good: the German was playing the game.

Taggart's voice from the periscope broke in upon Peter's concentration.

"Distant aircraft on the horizon, sir."

"Well, that settles it, Sub. I'll go deep now. Thirty metres!"

"Thirty metres, sir," the second coxswain repeated from the after planes as he spun his wheel. The boat reacted sharply, immediately adopting a bow-down angle.

Peter faced the depth gauges. Things were going well and so far events were normal: the German had decided to co-operate after all.

"Shut main vents," Peter ordered as she slid past fifteen metres.

"Shut main vents," growled the German in acknowledgement.

Eighteen metres, she was going down nicely, no bother at all. Peter heard the snapping of the vent levers as they were shut on the panel.

Then came a sudden increase of bow-down angle, and the depth started to leap downwards, twenty-five, thirty metres. At the same instant, Peter heard a scuffle behind him. There was a sharp *smack!*, a groan, and, as Peter spun round, the crumpled figure of the German slumped to the deck with Hawkins standing over him.

"The swine pulled this red-handled lever as well, sir," Hawkins shouted, his brawny hand pointing towards a red-painted lever, set slightly apart from the four main vent levers.

Peter had to act quickly. The boat was taking on a vicious angle and it was difficult to stand already.

"Take over the trim, Sub," he yelled. "The perisher has flooded Q and I'll have to find out how to blow it again. Pump like mad and speed up. You must hold her on the planes if you can."

But it was no use. The sudden flooding of the emergency tank at this depth — forty metres now — was too much for the planes, even at full speed.

When Peter jumped for the panel, Hawkins dragged the slumped body of the German away and shoved the limp form down the slope, so that it slithered against the for'd bulkhead of the Control Room, where it twitched for a few moments and then lay still.

Peter's thoughts raced. First, to shut the vent of the emergency tank. It *must* be this red lever! It now lay open, in a reverse position to the main vent levers, which he knew were in the shut position, for hadn't he just checked that?

He lunged for the lever and smacked it shut. He could hear no answering *thunk!* because of the noise of slithering bodies and the loose gear that clattered all about him in the confusion at this steep angle.

"I can't hold her, sir! Depth one hundred metres!" Taggart shouted desperately across the confined space.

Three hundred *feet?* In this split second of time, no, it couldn't be! Peter gasped as he saw the gauges: one hundred and twenty metres now — and the pointer racing round the dials. The planesmen were lying on the tilted deck and hanging on to the pipes for support. He had only a few seconds left in which to blow this tank, for they were out of control now and plunging to destruction. He groaned within himself — what a mess, oh God! What a fool he'd been to trust the German!

His eyes raced over the panel. Ah! there were the 'blows'. Little T-shaped valve spindles, just the same as *Rugged*'s. And there was one set slightly apart from the others, and yes! it was also painted red.

"This must be it!" he breathed as he yanked open the spindle. A high-pitched scream sang along the high-pressure line as the air tore along the pipe. Peter waited, tensed and hanging on to the panel, as his feet slid from under him. If he had guessed wrongly, not even the main vent 'blows' could save them now. He shut his eyes momentarily and prayed. Then he turned to watch the gauges — two hundred metres — six hundred feet, wasn't it, if his maths were correct? Surely it couldn't be? The boat had on a forty degree bow-down angle and the main motors — oh God, the main motors!

"Stop both!" he yelled.

Hawkins hauled himself to the doorway, painfully, agonisingly slowly.

"Stop both," he bellowed above the din.

From far away, they heard the tinkle of a bell and the lowering pitch in the whine of the motors.

Imperceptibly, so that it was a few seconds before Peter realised it, the angle gradually started to right itself.

He could stand upright now without holding on! A sigh whispered through the Control Room as the depth pointers steadied on two hundred and fifty metres — seven hundred and fifty feet! — and then she slowly pulled away from the depths.

Peter wrenched at the red-painted valve and stopped blowing. There was no need to advertise their position by blowing great gobs of air bubbles. Taggart and the planesmen had regained their positions and the boat was coming under control.

"Steady on fifty metres, Sub."

"Aye, aye, sir — fifty metres."

"I reckon we can do better on our own, don't you?" Peter asked. He was panting from his exertions, and a grin creased his sweating face. Now that the emergency was over he found that his hands were trembling, so he stuffed them in the pockets of his shorts.

"Don't want any more help from that stinking Hun, sir," Weston grunted from his after planes. "I reckon he's best where he is."

"Take him away, Hawkins. Tie him up and leave him in the Ward Room. We'll see to him later."

Hawkins' voice was low.

"Aye, aye, sir, but I'll break his neck if he tries anything again."

"He won't. I reckon you've broken his jaw in three places already!"

Bowles spoke up from the for'd planes.

"Hawkins weren't Med. Fleet champ for nothing, sir!"

Peter strode quickly through the boat, but in all compartments she had held. He'd always heard that the German U-boats could dive much deeper than our own, and now he believed it.

"All right, Flint?"

"Yes, sir, no water to speak of in the after ends."

"Good — it's Malta for us now!"

"Hope so, sir. This is too energetic!"

Peter returned to the Control Room and was glad to see that Taggart had taken charge and was trimming the boat satisfactorily.

After dark that night, U-93 surfaced off Cape Spartivento and started her charge without difficulty. At dawn twenty-four hours later, she surfaced off Filfla, the yellow walls of Malta glittering warmly in the sun.

It was strange to see the sinister silhouette of a U-boat entering the boom off Lazaretto, but at her standards a clean White Ensign fluttered bravely. Peter swallowed as he brought her to her buoys off Lazaretto, the cheers of *Rugged*'s company, in harbour two hours earlier, ringing in his ears.

Captain 'S' was awaiting him on the jetty, a broad smile on his kindly face.

"Well done, Sinclair," he said. "The sinking of U-93 by *Rugged* has already been announced by the B.B.C.!"

CHAPTER 10

Outmanoeuvred

"Start the attack!"

Peter was ashamed to feel his stomach sink when he heard Joe's command, an order that was now part of their daily existence. Each new attack secretly drained a trifle more of the reserve of self-control and courage from every man so that they wondered, deep down within themselves, how low their level of courage had fallen and how much reserve remained. It had not been so bad when they were new to this Mediterranean war — at least they knew that everything they met was hostile. But now the everlasting tension and lack of sleep were beginning to tell. No longer was the excitement exhilarating, no longer something of a novelty. They were tired, desperately tired, and they yearned for long, uninterrupted sleep. Judging by their faces, Peter saw that the breaking point could not be very far off; they were doing their duty like exhausted automatons and not as men with a will.

Peter sighed as he stumbled to his Diving Station between the depth gauges. It was too bad that they had not been given a night in harbour when they had returned with U-93. Instead, they had been ordered to transfer their gear immediately to *Rugged*. She had sailed again at dusk to take up the second billet in the Iron Ring, not off Taranto this time, but off Cape St. Vito.

Well, Captain 'S' knew best, thought Peter. *He'd never let them down yet, but did he realise how tired they all were?*

Peter automatically trimmed the boat while the attack developed. At the back of his mind he vaguely heard the Captain's routine orders. They had been on the billet now for two days, and fifteen minutes earlier, *Rapid*, the boat to the eastward of them and right under Cape St. Vito, had evidently fired and hit the cruiser that was making a sortie round the Cape.

Though *Rugged* was five miles away, she could hear the heat that *Rapid* was catching. The depth-charge explosions were clanging against *Rugged*'s pressure hull and were being chalked up by Saunders, the Outside E.R.A.

Joe had decided to go and see for himself. As usual there was a glassy calm 'up top', the surface of the sea a shining mirror. A periscope would be sighted miles away in these conditions, so Joe had been running deep and giving ten-minute bursts of full speed 'group-up'. At this rate the battery power would soon be exhausted and this was the eighth time that Peter had brought *Rugged* up from deep.

Peter looked at Joe. He was on all fours on the corticene deck, and using as little of the periscope as possible. The run-in had taken over an hour and the strain was beginning to tell.

"Don't break surface, for Pete's sake, Number One! Down periscope."

Joe snatched the sweat-rag that hung at his waist, and wiped it across his dripping brow.

"Aye, aye, sir," Peter replied wearily. This cat-and-mouse game from deep stretched nerves taut, because he had to settle her exactly on periscope-depth as the speed came off her.

"She's a cruiser all right," Joe continued, "she's low in the water aft, and steam and smoke is pouring from her, going straight upwards in the still air. Up periscope."

A quick swing round the horizon for aircraft, and he settled again on the target.

"She's got a whopper of a screen — one, two, three, four, five — Navigatoris — no, six — six Navigatoris, all weaving around her like wet hens!"

He slammed shut the handles and the periscope streaked downwards.

"Well, Number One, I daren't go deep and speed up any longer because I'm about twelve hundred yards off now. What's my course for a ninety track, Sub?"

"O-eight-two, sir."

"Port ten, steer o-eight-two."

"What's my D.A.?"

"Red two, sir."

"Put me on my D.A. Stand by all tubes! Up periscope."

Saunders carefully set the periscope on the D.A. and held the handles steady. Joe crouched low on the deck, cursing volubly.

"All tubes ready, sir."

"Stand by! Down periscope."

Joe swore again.

"There's an inquisitive aircraft coming our way. We'll have to be quick, Number One. Don't dip me now, for heaven's sake! Up periscope."

The tube hissed upwards once again, still held on the D.A. by Saunders.

"Fire one! … fire by time interval! Eighty feet, group-up, full ahead together," Joe's orders rapped out.

Peter took her down fast, and above the general activity he dimly heard Taggart's voice, "fire two — fire three — fire four! All tubes fired, sir."

Elliott nodded from his Asdic set.

"All torpedoes running, sir."

His head tilted on one side, Joe grinned as he listened for the explosion of the hits.

"Starboard twenty, steer o-nine-o and shut off from depth-charging."

There was an immediate *thump!* and the boat shook slightly.

"Our aviator friend," Joe said. "He dropped it where our tracks started, I'll bet, but he just gave us time though."

"Forty-five seconds, sir." Taggart reported the expected time when the torpedoes should hit and almost immediately there was a loud *clang!* striking the pressure hull.

"Group down, slow ahead port," Joe shouted above the cheer which echoed through the boat.

The counter-attack of the high-powered team escorting the cruiser was surprisingly ineffective. The bomb which the aircraft had dropped must have confused the attackers, for *Rugged* heard a concentrated attack developing astern of her, the explosions growing fainter as the distance increased. Then, twenty minutes later, Joe cautiously brought her to periscope depth.

"Hell's bells!" he swore. "A Navigatori has stopped our salvo. She must have crossed the tracks at the last moment — ah! there she goes, bows first and her stern cocked up in the air."

"Breaking-up noises, right astern, sir," Elliott chipped in.

"Thank you, Elliott. Down periscope. Number One, tell the Ship's Company we've sunk a Navigatori, but not the cruiser."

"Aye, aye, sir. Shall I open up from depth-charging?"

"Yes, please."

Although it was a disappointment not to have finished off the cruiser, a Navigatori was a sinking in which they took a peculiarly personal interest, for it made one less of their enemy to hunt them in the future.

When *Rugged* came to periscope depth at five o'clock, she received a signal recalling all the St. Vito Iron Ring to Malta, *Rugged* to retire first. She went deep to reload the remaining three torpedoes and set course to round up off Marittimo Island at dawn. Peter left his station between the gauges and wearily passed a hand across his face. It was five forty-five and he was not on watch until seven.

"Time for an hour's 'zizz'," he murmured as he went into the Ward Room to kick off his sandals and throw himself down on to his bunk. He rolled over to the ship's side and, with the comforting sounds of O'Riley laying up the supper things growing dimmer in his consciousness, he fell asleep.

It was seven o'clock when *Rugged* dived at dawn. The horizon to the eastward was green-streaked in a cold greyness and a silver haze hung low upon the horizon, a sure sign of another sweltering day.

Seven o'clock. The time is significant for it is a moment that has slashed a scar upon Peter's memory and which remains with him still. Seven o'clock was the time they dived and, for all they knew, it was to be another day of patrol routine — but a pleasant one because they were homeward-bound for Malta. They had dodged the E-boat patrol lines during the night and Joe had taken a good fix on Marittimo which placed them five miles to the southward of the island, the black pinnacle at the western extremity of the necklace of islets which reared ominously from the deeps.

So it was a slight shock when Peter heard from out of the corner of one ear, the summons that now made his stomach heave.

"Captain in the Control Room!"

Joe leapt from the Ward Room settee and snatched his spectacles from his nose. Without actually moving in his bunk, Peter was now fully awake and tensed for the next order which he knew was coming — ah, yes, here it was!

"Diving Stations!"

Peter dashed mechanically to his post between the gauges, while men stumbled to and fro to their stations throughout the boat.

"Start the attack! Bearing THAT, starboard fifteen, eighty feet, group up, half ahead together!"

The periscope handles snapped shut and the tube slithered downwards.

"Target — brand new trooper, ten thousand tons. Speed twenty knots. Escort — five destroyers, three weaving ahead. Stand by all tubes! What is my course for a sixty-track, Sub?"

A few seconds' delay while Taggart adjusted his Fruit Machine.

"Three-four-five, sir. D.A. Green twelve."

And so once more another attack developed — a snap attack and all over in twelve minutes, *Rugged* coming up from deep when the first destroyer had thundered overhead. Joe fired from inside the weaving screen, and as the three torpedoes sped from the tubes, *Rugged* went deep to one hundred and twenty feet, turning hard on her heel at the same instant.

It was a classic attack. The enemy hardly knew what had hit them until it was too late. Joe's last glimpse through the periscope was of a vast white wall of ship's side, and a streaming wisp from the nearest destroyer's siren as she desperately tried to warn the trooper of the approaching torpedo tracks. Then two torpedoes tore into the trooper, smack amidships, the explosions slapping *Rugged*'s pressure hull like steam hammers.

Joe grinned.

"No doubt about that, Number One! Now for home, as we've no fish left. Group down, stop starboard, and stay at one hundred and twenty feet. Steer one-two-o — I'll try and slip away, straight for Piccadilly."

But reaching Piccadilly was not so simple in spite of the high hopes from their initial success. Ten minutes had elapsed since the torpedoes had struck home. Elliott had just reported continued breaking-up noises from the stricken ship which spiralled down into the depths, her bulkheads and tanks collapsing under the pressure. So it was all the more of a disappointment when Elliott reported H.E. fine on the starboard bow, and destroyer H.E. at that.

Well, here we go, thought Peter, *just our luck to catch the heat at the last moment.*

Joe glanced towards him.

"Shut off from depth-charging, Number One."

The bulkhead doors swung to ponderously, the black-handled clips moved by unseen hands from the other side of the bulkhead, so that each compartment was now tightly sealed, a small world on its own.

It was exactly ten-thirty in the morning when the first destroyer gained contact.

"Silent routine, starboard ten," Joe ordered, as a curious feeling of apprehension swamped him, like a mist which rolls in from the sea.

The submarine swung slowly end-on to her hunter.

"Steady."

"One-six-o, sir," the helmsman reported.

Elliott looked up from his set.

"Destroyer in contact, red eight-five, sir."

Peter instinctively cocked his head on one side, listening for the Asdic pulses: yes, there they were! He could hear them now, very faint but gradually intensifying.

Tick-tick-tick, tick-tick…

"Starboard ten," Joe ordered, a look of anger on his lined face, a face beginning to show the strain of these last ten days. The stubble of his beard darkly accentuated the gaunt features, so that the highlights in his eyes flickered restlessly as he glanced at the barometer above Peter's head.

"What's the pressure showing, Number One?"

High-pressure air is used to discharge torpedoes from their tubes, and in order to prevent this air escaping to the surface and betraying their position, it is always vented inboard, back into the submarine. Inevitably this builds up the pressure inside the boat, and, what with other air leaks and the venting of 'Q' tank inboard, the air pressure in the boat had increased considerably.

"Three inches, sir."

Joe nodded — the pressure was high already. Ah well, it had often been higher, and when they surfaced tonight for a charge the pressure would be released as the hatch opened. He looked at the clock: ten-thirty-five, and now the second destroyer was running in to attack.

"Five hundred yards, sir," Elliott reported quietly.

"Starboard twenty; don't speed up, Number One."

Peter tried to hold her on the planes, but, with this amount of rudder, she slipped down twelve feet. The last minute alteration, however, threw the attacker off the scent and the pattern burst harmlessly astern of them, wide on the starboard quarter, not even dislodging cork from the deckhead.

"Ship's head?" asked the Captain.

"Two-four-o, sir."

"Steady. Steer two-four-o."

As the rumble and clatter of the water noises died away, the sinister tick-ticking from the Asdic impulses of the destroyer in contact pervaded the boat once more.

"Another destroyer in contact, Green two-o, sir." Joe rubbed his chin pensively.

"Umm — how many destroyers can you make out, Elliott?"

The H.S.D. methodically carried out an all-round listening-sweep, while all eyes in the Control Room watched his hands sensitively turning the ebonite knobs. Then he slowly straightened his back.

"Five, sir. All equally spaced around us in a circle."

"Ha! Must be the Trapani First Eleven, Number One. We've got some opposition this time."

Peter turned round to face his Captain, a smile on his face, but with a sinking in his stomach.

"Yes, sir, and I bet they're mad at losing their troop transport. Rommel could have done with those squareheads."

So now they were for it! They were encircled by five of the Trapani team, the most respected of all the enemy destroyers. The Fighting Tenth knew them of old, an efficient and remorseless destroyer group which hunted as a team, with too frequent success: the losses in the flotilla were largely due to the Trapani First Eleven.

Up above, the hunters saturated the circle with depth charges, and it was perhaps for this reason that the trapped submarine managed to survive the holocaust. The water was so convulsed that the operators in the hunting ships were having difficulty in maintaining contact. Keeping end-on to her pursuers, *Rugged* twisted and turned until she reached the perimeter of the circle, but always, just as she was slipping through the net, she would be picked up again.

Joe looked at the clock which was still functioning — a sure sign of inaccurate attacks, for it always stopped when the patterns were close. Only six o'clock, near as dammit. How these hours had dragged, with already seven-and-a-half hours of intensive depth-charging! Joe sat on a stool, his back leaning against the for'd periscope. He could concentrate in comfort here, and, heaven knows, he could do with some rest. A sardonic grin spread across his tired face.

"What's the score so far, Saunders?"

The Outside E.R.A. sat on his toolbox, and across his knees was spread a large sheet of paper covered with crosses and timings.

"One hundred and thirty-six, sir."

"Well, at this rate, they can't have many depth charges left, sir," Peter interjected hopefully.

"Trapani isn't far away, and they can always send out reliefs," Joe replied. "On a flat-calm like this, they ought to be able to keep in contact all night. It will be interesting to see what happens at dusk."

Benson spoke up from the Chart Table.

"Twilight's at seven o'clock, sir."

Joe nodded, but he was watching Elliott who was concentrating on his dial, a mug of lime juice hastily thrust to one side. He had now been closed up for eleven hours, but then, when he spoke, his voice was as imperturbable as ever.

"Red six-o, sir. Destroyer running in to attack."

In the fore-ends the Torpedo Instructor, Petty Officer Rodney Slater, lay full stretch upon the corticene, his head propped against the narrow partition between the tube-space doors that were now clipped shut. For a long time now he had been half listening to the desultory conversation that was being bandied about the compartment. From the open hatch that led down into the cramped quarters of the pump space, the burly shoulders of Stoker O'Connor sprawled, his black hair tousled across his face, so pouchy and pale with its lack of fresh air and sleep. He was carrying on a hoarse dialogue with Ordinary Seaman Smith, the T.I.'s Mate, as he was known. Smith sprawled under the empty port racks, while Hawkins and O'Riley slept fitfully upon the oily corticene on the opposite side.

Slater idly watched a couple of cockroaches crawling in their jerky movements across O'Riley's face. The seaman instinctively blew from his lower lip but, failing to dislodge the pests, his hand flapped listlessly to brush them off. Overhead Slater could hear the whistling of the fore-planes as they shuddered from the movement induced by the fore-planesman in the Control Room.

He looked at his watch while another destroyer rumbled overhead, its propellers churning the waters in a weird cacophony. A pause, and then the boat jumped to the shock of the depth-charges which clanged against the pressure hull.

It was six-thirty and Slater, by now, was past caring. In his sensitive mind, he knew that this time they were really up against it: eight hours' depth-charging and still no sign of an abatement. Smith was talking, and it was the harsh grating of his voice that made Slater suddenly prick up his ears.

"I'm fed up with it, Stokes, I tell you," Smith was saying, "press-ganged into this outfit and what d'you get?"

O'Connor stared at him but remained silent, while Smith continued, with rising voice, "Eight hours' heat, that's all you get, with the prospect of another eight."

"We sank a trooper, Smithy," O'Connor chipped in.

"Yeah, one bleedin' little trooper. What good'll that do in this flamin' war? The Ol' Man's nuts; he should 'a let that one go," he went on, "we were on our way 'ome, weren't we?" and he looked aggressively around the silent fore-ends.

The bulk of Able Seaman Hawkins stirred under the racks and O'Riley shifted his weight in his sleep.

Slater stood up.

"Say that again, Smith."

"The Old Man's nuts and he should have let the trooper alone."

"Dry up!"

Slater moved towards the overstrained seaman, his hands clenched. Smith remained on the deck, a look of insolence upon his face. He started to speak but decided that discretion was the better part of valour.

A worried man, Slater returned to his position at the for'd end of the compartment. It was the first time that he'd seen signs of cracking in one of his men.

Half an hour before midnight, a lull came in the attacks. The Captain decided to open up from depth-charging, and it was a relief when the bulkhead doors swung open again.

"Remind the ship's company that we are still at Silent Routine, Number One — we're still being hunted."

For twenty minutes there had been no attacks. No one in contact, no Asdic pulses, no propeller noises, nothing.

"Well, Number One, it looks as if our luck's in. If we're clear in half an hour I'll surface and that would give us at least five hours' charging. What's the pressure?"

"Four and a half inches, sir."

"Thought so. It's about time we got some fresh air."

Four and a half inches was a large pressure — too much, for already the air was foul and stuffy. It would be good to get up, and what a mercy it was to have slipped away from their hunters.

"Stand by to surface!"

Twenty minutes later, *Rugged* slid silently up from deep to periscope depth. The lookouts and the signalman were in the tower while Joe had a rapid all-round look in high-power.

"Plane up to the surface on main motors only. Do not blow main ballast until I give the order, but start the blowers now. Surface!"

"Group up, half ahead together. Both planes to rise. Start the blowers," Peter ordered.

The Captain leapt up the ladder and Peter heard the signalman grappling with the clips.

"Fifteen feet, sir!"

Swoosh! A rush of air swept by Peter as the pressure was released through the conning tower.

"Stop both!" the order came faintly from the tower.

Joe found himself panting from the extra air, and, if he had not hung on to the signalman's ankles, the release of pressure would have catapulted the man over the side. The water still drenched blackly down the bridge-side, spilling through the free-flood holes. Joe picked up his glasses for a quick sweep, but, as he did so, he glanced over the side.

He could never remember afterwards who was the more surprised, the enemy or himself. He had surfaced alongside the low silhouette of an E-boat which was only twenty yards clear, where she lay stopped and listening. An Italian stood rooted to the upper deck, a cigarette glowing redly from his mouth. Joe distinctly saw him grasp the guard rail for support, shake himself, and then give a howl of astonishment while he frantically pointed with outstretched arm.

"Dive, dive, dive!" yelled Joe as he jumped down the hatch on top of the signalman who had preceded him. From the corner of his eye he saw the black outlines of two destroyers, motionless and waiting. Joe had walked right into the baited trap and now the spring was sprung. He swore as he pulled down the upper lid upon him.

"Now we're for it!" he whispered.

CHAPTER 11

"... And Twenty Minutes"

The hands of the Ward Room clock were groping for three a.m. *Rugged* had miraculously escaped the renewed counter-attacks, in spite of the fact that the enemy were now doubly incensed. They threw everything they had at her, but Joe made no false move and the boat was as silent as doom itself. Although she twisted and turned, she remained trapped within the circle.

Peter had six complicated graphs spread out before him on the Ward Room table. Joe sat facing him, his long fingers drumming on the mahogany. Taggart was on watch in the Control Room, while Benson navigated.

"Well, Number One, what's the score?" Joe demanded quietly.

"I've double checked, sir, and Flint has taken check readings of the densities. At a speed of slow ahead one propeller, I reckon that the batteries have eighteen hours' life left in them."

"Only eighteen hours at slow one?"

"Yes, sir, that's all."

"That takes us up to nine p.m. tonight."

"Allowing for no other electrical consumption, sir, such as the galley, lighting and running the pumps."

Joe lowered his voice.

"This is serious, Number One. We have only two hours' darkness left in which to surface and get in our charge. But how the devil can I with those destroyers up top. Listen—"

There was no need to cock their ears, for the tick-ticking of the Asdic impulses was all around them.

"What about air then?" Joe asked, truculent in his weariness.

"Luckily the pressure was released when you opened the hatch for a second or two," Peter continued, "but the air's foul. We've had nearly twenty-four hours dived already."

"I know that, but we've done twenty-four hours before."

"Yes, sir, once; but never thirty-six."

"When does that take us to, then?"

"Sunset tonight."

"Sunset — the next chance of surfacing."

" — if we've thrown off the hunters, sir."

And so the conference continued, and slowly the truth sunk in upon their tired minds.

"I've had no experience in a boat of this small size, Number One, never as long as thirty-six hours. But we might be all right for carbon dioxide poisoning if we use the Protosorb."

Peter was silent for a moment.

"We left it in the dockyard, sir, during our last refit," Peter went on quietly. "Don't you remember? We decided it took up too much room with all the trays — you said it was useless stuff anyway."

Joe controlled himself, the muscles of his gaunt face working spasmodically. In this bitter hour of defeat, Peter would remember him, valiant in adversity.

"Well, Peter," Joe said at last, for the first time addressing him by his Christian name, "you're the second-in-command and I want your opinion. You know the decision we have got to make?"

"Yes, sir, I do."

"Well, what's it to be?"

"Stick it out, sir. See it through until sunset, whatever the effects of lack of oxygen and carbon dioxide poisoning might be."

"You know what the effects are?"

"I have a pretty good idea, sir, from the pre-war American films."

Joe chuckled bitterly.

"You know the effect it may have on the crew?"

"Not our ship's company, sir."

"We can't lie on the bottom for it's too deep."

"No, sir."

Joe paused a full minute.

"The only other course open to us is to surface at dawn and fight it out."

"With our pop-guns against five destroyers — just to be machine-gunned as we crawl out. We can always do that later, sir."

" — and those of us who survive to spend the rest of the war in the Bag," Joe continued dreamily. "No thanks; I'm glad you think as I do, Peter, for I agree with everything you've said."

Then, for him, Joe Croxton did a strange thing. He stood up and held his hand out to Peter across the Ward Room table.

"Thank you, Peter. When we get out of this, it will be something to remember, won't it?"

Peter took the proffered hand, but he was unable to speak. He slowly replaced the graphs in the drawer, then he followed his Captain back into the Control Room.

It was now four in the morning, and for a short space the counter-attacks had decreased in frequency. The ship's company had been at Diving Stations for twenty-two hours, but before settling down for the long ordeal, Joe Croxton decided to walk through the boat to explain the situation in his own way. In each compartment, a small group of men huddled around the tall figure who explained matters so simply: surface in an hour's time to fight it out against overwhelming odds, or carry out an uncontrolled experiment in endurance by seeing whether they could stay alive in this atmosphere for another fourteen hours.

In the fore-ends, there was a murmur of assent from all save Smith who peered resolutely at the deck and said nothing. The Engine Room and Motor Room crews fully understood, and then Joe sent them all to Watch Diving.

"We'll do four-hour tricks instead of two," he said, "to minimise movement and conserve oxygen. All hands are to turn in and to save oxygen there is to be no talking or eating. There will be no meals until this is over, and I know I can count on you to see that these orders are obeyed implicitly — all our lives depend upon that."

Joe camped down again in the Control Room to counter the moves of the hunters with the minimum of physical effort. Benson took over the Watch while Peter and Taggart turned into their bunks.

Peter suddenly realised that he was panting from the exertion of climbing over his bunk-board. He lay still and watched his chest heaving while his lungs craved for air. He looked at his watch: seven in the morning, and how long to go before sunset? Twelve hours! He was already suffering from lack of oxygen, so what would it be like in twelve hours' time and after the effects of carbon dioxide had made themselves felt? He crossed his arms under his head and stared at the sweating pipes that dripped four inches above his face. He could just hear the propeller beats of a destroyer, which had run over their stern, fading down the port side.

His thoughts were interrupted by a gentle tapping on the Ward Room table and by a discreet cough.

"First Lieutenant, sir."

Peter turned on one side to see the small figure of Chief E.R.A. Potts, standing in the passage.

"Yes, Chief?"

"The Captain wants to start on the oxygen now, sir. I haven't any pressure gauges in my stores for the cylinders, and I was wondering if by any chance you knew of any?"

In the rush of leaving England for Malta, these six gauges had been overlooked. The chances of their ever being required seriously had been too remote to bother about anyway. Peter slowly shook his head.

"Sorry, Chief, I haven't any. You'll just have to crack the valves on each cylinder and guess the amount."

The Chief paused.

"Yes, sir, that's what I'm afraid of: I shan't know how much oxygen there will be left after each issue."

"You'll just have to judge it and chance it. Shall I help you with it, Chief?" and Peter started to crawl from his bunk.

"It's all right. I'll do it, sir, you've been on your feet for twenty-four hours, so leave it to me."

"Thanks, Chief."

The blue-jowled face had disappeared for'd, and his shuffling feet could be heard slip-slapping towards the fore-ends. Peter slumped back on to his bunk where he lay sweating on top of the one coarse blanket. This latest movement made him breathe deeply, long and deliberately, so that he could feel the life-giving air reaching to the depths of his lungs. Slowly his breathing became normal, but even then he realised that every intake was a deliberate, conscious effort. Previously he had never noticed that his lungs moved as he inhaled, but now the action was prolonged, deliberate. How much longer of this? Seven-thirty? It must be later! But no, his watch was right. A glorious sunrise must just be dawning upon their hunters overhead; green and silver-shot it most probably was. He shut his eyes to savour the beauty in his imagination, and then slowly the realisation came to him that a slow, dull ache was spreading across his forehead, a rhythmical pounding that throbbed in time with his heartbeat.

He opened his eyes as the truth struck him. Seven thirty only, and already carbon dioxide poisoning was having its effect. He tried to blink away the dull ache, but it remained. Yes, CO_2 already! He groaned inwardly: they hadn't a chance with twelve hours to go, not a chance.

"May I, sir?"

"Yes, of course, Chief."

The oxygen cylinder was above the Captain's settee. About four feet long and six inches in diameter, it was slung on the deckhead, just above the pistol locker. How pitifully inadequate it looked, and there was only one in each compartment! The Chief stood on his toes upon the settee, and carefully inserted his wheel spanner; a gentle pull, a ten second hiss, the clatter of the spanner as it was removed, and then Peter relaxed the full length of his body as the life-giving oxygen reached his lungs. The relief was exquisite; he could take a long breath to the very depths of his body, and he was satisfied, completely at peace. And for eight whole glorious minutes this was so — seven forty-two? Only twelve minutes since the last look: he would have to ration himself at glancing at the time or it would never pass. Then he felt the insistent demand of his lungs again, dragging at the inadequate air. The ache across his brows had not disappeared with the oxygen, but what did that matter so long as he could look forward to another ration of oxygen later?

He turned on his left side to search for sleep: that would be the quickest way to shorten this agony. But in this position his lungs protested, so that he slumped on to his back again, clamouring for air. As he did so, he saw Benson smiling at him from his bunk on the opposite side of the table. But, though he smiled with his mouth, Peter could see fear showing starkly in his eyes.

Poor chap, thought Peter, *he's as scared as I am.*

"Number One?" Benson's whisper floated across the Ward Room.

"Don't talk, Pilot. Save your breath."

"We haven't got a chance, have we?"

Peter could see the intelligent eyes accusing him, terrified eyes that betrayed their fear.

"Answer me, Number One."

Peter looked at him long and hard.

"Shut up, Pilot. Don't be so blasted pessimistic and get some sleep. We'll get out of this."

The black eyes left him and the lithe body turned over on its side to face the bulkhead. Peter watched the heaving figure sadly. Were the shoulders shaking for lack of air?

Oh, my God, Peter prayed, *in Thy mercy, save us from a horrible death.* He closed his eyes and merciful oblivion swept over him, as he fell into an uneasy sleep.

Joe Croxton dragged his tired eyes away from the compass to look at the clock. Three-fifteen in the afternoon. Heavens, how the time was dragging! The crew were beginning to show the effects of the CO_2 poisoning now, and things were becoming dangerous. Only five minutes ago, Number One, who was now on watch, had ordered the pump space operator to pump on 'Q' and O'Connor had flooded instead. Fortunately, Number One detected it immediately, or it could have been disastrous. That was the danger of this lack of oxygen and CO_2 poisoning: a man would swear that two and two made five and act accordingly. He would open a valve, swearing that he had shut it, and genuinely believe that he had. Things were getting dangerous.

This unending day had taken on a nightmarish quality. Men lay semi-conscious in their bunks, waiting for the Chief to appear upon his oxygen rounds. The hiss of the escaping gas would jerk awake those fortunate enough to have found sleep, and they would lie gasping for life-giving air like beached trout upon the pebbles of a Scottish burn. Floundering there in their sweltering bunks, or panting in corners on the oily corticene, they would be kept from sleep by the sudden shriek and spate of gibberish from a gabbling sleeper, moaning in his nightmare. Like some horrid dream, the hours became unreal, dragging interminably while the hands of the clocks stood still.

Each man reacted differently under the effects of the CO_2 poisoning and the lack of oxygen. On some, the effects were limited to excruciating headaches, vomiting and sweating. But on others the sands of time were running out.

Young Keating twisted his head round the Engine Room bulkhead door, and without raising himself from his squatting position, his mouth opened mechanically beneath frightened eyes.

"Captain, sir. Somefink funny's happened to the L.T.O. in the Motor Room."

"What's up?"

"He wants help, sir."

"Watch the boat, Number One. I'm going aft."

Joe reached the Motor Room to find a stoker bending over and trying to console Leading Seaman Flint, who sat propped against the stanchion by the switchboard.

"He can't move, sir," the stoker said.

Joe put his arm gently around the young man's shoulders and tried to lift him, but the legs and arms were strangely rigid. From beneath his dark hair, the eyes swivelled to follow Joe's movements, but the head could not turn.

"Can you speak, Flint?"

A gabble croaked from lips that remained immobile. The terrified eyes met his Captain's and pleaded for reassurance. The heat was stifling between the switchboards and Joe gasped, gently patting the young man's shoulder.

"It's all right, old chap, it's only heat exhaustion. We'll take you for'd to your mess."

The horror of Flint's plight had scared the stoker, but now, since Joe had used up so much of his energy to come and see Flint specially, the L.T.O.'s terror vanished from his face, a gabble of gratitude croaking from his throat.

"Watch him while I get a relief sent aft."

Joe reached the Control Room and slumped down by the Fruit Machine where he lay gasping for breath before he could speak.

"Number One — have Flint relieved, then take him to his bunk: he's paralysed. I'll stay here and watch the boat."

"Aye, aye, sir."

With two volunteers, Peter lugged the paralysed man for'd to his bunk in the Petty Officers' Mess. Gently forcing Flint's lips apart, he trickled half a cup of lime juice down the parched throat and then he felt the sweating brow.

"Don't worry, Flint, you'll soon be all right."

Was he wrong, or when he turned on his heel for the Control Room, did Peter detect a glimmer of amusement in the paralysed man's eyes?

Peter sat in the Ward Room, slumped over the table, his head cradled in his crossed arms. He couldn't afford the air to climb back into his bunk, and he found that the throbbing in his skull hurt less in this position. He had just been relieved by Taggart, and he had been only too thankful to take the weight off his leaden legs. His chest heaved, his ears throbbed and a faint muzziness had crept into his vision. A voice from far away wafted into his consciousness.

"Are you listening, Number One?"

It was Benson, the Pilot, wasn't it? Peter lifted his head and forced a smile. Benson was on the settee, resting on one arm.

"Yes, Pilot."

"They are still in contact," Benson whispered.

"Yes."

"And there's still two hours to go before twilight?"

"Yes," Peter replied gruffly, for he was trying to conserve his breath, "if you've got your time of sunset right."

Benson's face was strung taut, mask-like, two glittering eyes darting at Peter.

"I'm bringing up blood now, Number One."

"You're not the only one."

"But," Benson gasped, a crimson-dyed handkerchief clutched in his hand, "I can't breathe now: how the devil can we last another two hours?"

Peter did not immediately reply, for he felt his self-control slipping, a surge of anger sweeping over him, so that he could have struck Benson in his feebleness. It was a pity, in the circumstances, that he did not lash out for it might have helped the young Navigator.

When the mist cleared from Peter's eyes, he saw that Benson had rolled on his side.

"Oh, for heaven's sake, Pilot, pull yourself together," Peter whispered.

The shoulders shook, and from the settee choking sobs broke the silence. Peter swept round the end of the table and wrenched the man's shoulders back.

"Shut up, Pilot, for Pete's sake."

Benson's mouth hung open as the sobs wracked the contorted body, and from the corner of his mouth a slender crimson line slowly welled.

Suddenly anger flowed into compassion, for there are moments when humanity replaces iron discipline. Peter hove the shoulders upright and it was at this moment that the Captain groped into the Ward Room.

"What's up?"

"Pilot's not so hot, sir."

"What's the matter?"

"He's taking it worse than most, sir. His nerve—"

Joe's eyes were granite as he stared across at the wretched Navigator.

"Do what you can for him, Number One — and don't let the troops know."

The horrible spluttering slowly subsided, as Peter made him comfortable.

Then Peter suddenly realised the significance of the Captain's presence in the Ward Room — the counter-attacks had tailed off, there could be no other explanation. Peter looked at Joe.

The Captain nodded.

"They're not in contact."

A smile slowly spread across Peter's face.

"But they may still be listening, Number One; remember?"

Peter's smile changed to a grin.

"But it's five-thirty, sir, and only another hour and a half?"

Joe grimaced.

"It's going to be touch-and-go."

There was a discreet cough in the passage and the grave face of the Coxswain looked in.

"The Chief's passed out, sir."

Joe's head jerked up, his eyes questioning.

"He's all right, sir. I've put him in his bunk."

"Thank you, Cox'n. The First Lieutenant will continue with the oxygen."

The Coxswain smiled.

"It's not much use now, sir."

Joe nodded and looked up at the wise face that peered down with such understanding upon his young Captain.

"But tell the hands, Cox'n, that the destroyers appear to have lost contact and that we shall be surfacing, God willing, in ninety minutes' time."

"Aye, aye, sir; thank you, sir," and the Coxswain disappeared for'd.

Joe looked at Peter.

"Off you go, Number One. Give the Ward Room its oxygen last: it's no good anyway!"

The reek of the torpoil in the fore-ends had been too much for O'Riley. He lay gasping in the corner, his head over a bucket. The T.I. reeled over to him and with rough tenderness held the heaving shoulders.

"All right, Jock?"

The Glasgow seaman nodded before another spasm shook him.

In the starboard corner, Ordinary Seaman Smith had been brooding for the past two hours, but now his tongue had become unloosed and a flow of abuse poured forth, directed at O'Riley. The wretched Scot turned towards his messmate, bewilderment upon his hurt face.

"Turn it up, Smith," the T.I. snapped. "Jock can't help it."

"No, he can't perishin' well help it," Smith continued, an edge tainting his voice, "but our Mister perishin' Croxton could. The silly blighter got us into this."

The voice shrilled in the silence, echoing in the confined space. Smith was standing up now, his hands clenched and held out before him, almost in a gesture of supplication, pathetic to watch.

Hawkins had been panting by the bulkhead door, but now he strode up to Smith.

"Shut up, ye blasted fool!" and he gripped Smith by the frail shoulders. The sudden action snapped the finely drawn tension that exists in a man's brain, the razor's edge over which we suddenly stumble unwittingly. A wild light blazed in Smith's eyes as he lashed out at Hawkins.

"Take your filthy hands off me, you creepin' crawler," the voice shrieked shrilly. "Get away from me. We can't get out. We're trapped, I tell you, trapped," and a small froth of whiteness bubbled at the corner of his mouth as he continued incoherently, "I want to see the Old Man. Let me through, blast ye, let me through!"

The T.I. stood by the bulkhead door. He watched the insane Smith try to struggle past Hawkins' vast bulk. Hawkins turned towards Slater, while he held off Smith's writhing body with one arm.

"Shall I, T.I.?" Hawkins pleaded in a whisper.

Slater nodded.

There was a sharp *click!* and Smith folded up to slide unconscious to the deck.

"Excuse me, T.I..."

Slater spun round. He stood aside to allow the First Lieutenant into the fore-ends.

There was the fraction of a pause as the First Lieutenant took in the scene.

"Where's the oxygen bottle?" he asked.

Hawkins, who seemed to be gasping for air more energetically than the others and whose immense bulk was vainly trying to conceal the huddled body, pointed to the cylinder behind Peter's head.

"It's up there, sir."

Peter turned round and took an unconsciously long time in fumbling with the valve. There was a long hiss, and without turning round he left the fore-ends.

"Thank you," he said. "We shall be surfacing in an hour's time."

Six-thirty, and it was the last half hour which dragged the longest in this hideous nightmare. The air seemed utterly intangible: there was nothing for the lungs to grip as men lay gasping, taking in long, long draughts of nothingness, stretching their chests so that they could feel the very depths of their bellows. And so it continued, thirty minutes of unmitigated torture.

But at last the black hands of the clock in the Control Room crept to seven o'clock. As the second hand crossed the hour, Taggart reported to the Captain in the Ward Room.

"Seven o'clock, sir."

Joe looked up.

"Go to Diving Stations."

"Aye, aye, sir."

When Taggart's figure had gone, Joe went over to Benson's horizontal figure, now turned to the bulkhead in shame.

"Come on, Pilot," the Captain gently said.

Benson turned on his back, the eyes questioning, a whisper which was barely audible escaping from his lips.

"So sorry, sir."

Joe paused as he looked down at the deathly paleness of the young man.

"That's all right," he said gently. "Come on now, you're wanted."

The wracked body slowly rose from the bunk, paused as it coughed in agonised gasps, then hove its way to the wire mesh of the gyro panel.

O'Connor's burly figure was shambling aft and, in an unselfconscious gesture, his strong arm encircled the gasping officer to help him to his position at the chart table.

"Thanks, O'Connor."

"Sure, that's foine, sorr," and he continued stumbling his way aft.

Joe waited five minutes while Elliott carried out a careful all-round sweep. The tension sizzled in the silence, for the slightest suspicion of an enemy on the surface now meant that they must fight it out when they broke surface. But they were prepared to take on the whole Italian battle-fleet if need be: it would be a sweet and merciful death compared to this. But had they the strength to man the guns, not that it mattered anyway?

"No H.E., sir."

A sigh rustled gently through the Control Room.

"Stand by to surface."

It took ten minutes for Peter to be satisfied, for three garbled reports had to be verified: they could not afford mistakes now, with men's minds wandering.

"Ready to surface, sir."

"Periscope depth!"

At last! Thirty-six hours, thirty-six hours of indescribable horror. It mattered nothing if all the enemy destroyers in the world were waiting for them, at least they would get air — air, that God-sent gift which they had previously taken for granted.

Rugged swooped upwards, sixty, forty, thirty feet.

"Twenty-eight feet, sir!" Peter sang out, his knees buckling beneath him, as he unconsciously but ridiculously tried to hold her at her depth. He felt the periscope swish upwards, and then he heard Joe panting as he swung the glass around the horizon.

"Eighty feet!" Joe gasped.

Men groaned audibly, and even the Cox'n took his eyes off his bubble to peer at the Captain's face. So they were to die! Now they knew what 'hunted to exhaustion' meant! Well, they didn't want any more of it and were ready to die. They'd done their best, dammit, so better get it over with, quickly…

"Eighty feet, sir," Peter replied, his hand trembling uncontrollably as he flicked the pump-order instrument. So it was to be gun action after all! For a second he turned to face his Captain.

Joe was smiling. He had left the periscope up, and he stood with his arms hanging limply over the handles for support.

"Nothing in sight, Number One, not a sausage! But it's still daylight!"

A loud sigh whispered through the boat. Another agonising twenty minutes, but there was no one in sight! They could stick another twenty minutes, knowing that. No one in sight... Men thumped each other on the back, shook hands, and smiled. So they had almost made it ... another twenty minutes would make it certain.

It was the longest twenty minutes of Peter's life, the most excruciating, the most nerve-racking. They all watched Elliott as he continued with his listening watch; he only had to pick something up and...

But Elliott remained silent and twenty minutes later they surfaced. Peter stood at the bottom of the ladder as the hatch opened; the air-pressure swooshed by him, and in the red lighting and in the silence they wallowed and waited for the order that was to bring them relief: "Start the generators!"

Peter waited. He looked at the clock. Three minutes had gone and still no sign from the bridge. The voicepipe cock had not even been opened, for the helmsman's ready bucket was still empty. There was something wrong!

"Nip up top and make your report, Navigating Officer."

Benson lunged for the ladder and they listened as his feet stumbled upwards. Peter peeped upwards into the dark abyss, and seconds later he heard the distant voice of the pilot.

"Control Room! They've all passed out — they're unconscious on the bridge."

But suddenly a gush of water spurted down the voicepipe, and Peter knew that all was well. The flush of oxygen in the fresh air had been too much for the bridge personnel; they had lost consciousness and were hanging limply over the bridge.

And so the generators were started at last! A stream of life-giving fresh air was sucked down the conning tower by the diesels as they spluttered into life. It was the most exquisite moment in all their lives. Peter allowed groups of men to come in turn around the lower lid, and they stood there, gulping in the glorious stuff, singing and clapping each other on the back. Some had tears streaming down their faces.

Joe took a fix on a dark pinnacle that jutted from the sea: Marittimo! They were still within five miles of the position where they had first started the attack!

Fifteen minutes later, they were put down by an attacking Wellington that lumbered overhead. The bombs went wide, and *Rugged* surfaced light-heartedly to set course for Malta. They were already twenty-four hours overdue.

CHAPTER 12

Alexandrian Interlude

"Hullo, George!"

Paymaster Sub-Lieutenant George Morris took little notice of the greeting and continued working at his ledger. His mind must be playing him tricks for his friend, Peter Sinclair, had become overdue yesterday in *Rugged*. Part-owner of a dinghy with Sinclair, their friendship had developed, and the news of *Rugged*'s loss was a deep wound in George Morris's soul; he had lost a good friend.

"Hullo, George, you old rascal!"

The 'Pay' swung round on his stool and there, standing before him, was Peter Sinclair grinning all over his grey face. George Morris slowly stretched out his hand to touch the apparition.

"My God, Peter, I thought you were dead!" and the 'Pay' let out a long-drawn sigh.

Peter thumped him on the back, so that the wretched Paymaster Sub-Lieutenant dropped his inky pen upon the ledger.

"Very nearly; but not quite, George."

"When d'you get in?"

"Half an hour ago. How's the dinghy?"

"Fine shape. How about sailing over to St. Paul's Bay tomorrow, after you've had your sleep?"

"Yes, let's. I'd like to get away for a spell."

But it was not to be and instead, *Rugged* was sent up to Torpedo Creek to reload for her next patrol. She refuelled, stored and was ready for sea by the following evening. Flint had recovered from his paralysis, and, although they were dog-tired, it was surprising how quickly the ship's company recuperated. Two hours before sailing, Captain 'S' addressed them in the courtyard.

"Well, *Rugged*, you'll hate this, I know. You won't like leaving the rest of us for a month, but we'll try to keep it going while you're away," and a twinkle appeared momentarily in the wise eyes. Peter felt his heart beating faster: what was coming now?

"I reckon," Captain 'S' continued, "that you deserve a rest, and I'm sending you off on a quiet billet. Your patrol will take you to Alexandria for a couple of days, and then on to the Fourth Flotilla at Beirut where you will all have fourteen days' leave up in their rest camp in the hills — skiing and all that!" Was it a hallucination or could Peter see grins on the faces of those in the rear rank?

"Thank you, *Rugged*; God-speed and come back fresh and rearing to go," and the jovial figure turned on his heel to leave the courtyard.

"Ship's Company, 'shun!" Joe's voice barked unfamiliarly, "turn right, dis—miss!"

Rugged slipped at dusk. Fading into the twilight, her sleek and rust-splotched outline was followed by the envious eyes of the spare crew remaining in Lazaretto.

"Lucky beggars!" a sailor's voice growled from the jetty.

"Reckon they've deserved it, mate," his messmate replied.

After five uneventful days and nights, *Rugged* surfaced off the swept channel to Alexandria harbour, where a sweeper waited to escort her into the dockyard. The ship's company were in high spirits as they secured alongside the unfamiliar jetties.

"Proper skylark, ain't it, Bill?" Ordinary Seaman Smith jocularly remarked in the fore-ends. He was now fully recovered, and except for a purple blotch encircling his left eye, there was nothing to remind him of the episode now ten days old: all was forgiven and forgotten.

Hawkins was squaring up his gear and trying to find his shaving things.

"Going ashore tonight, Smithy?" he asked jauntily.

"What d'ya take me for, Bill? 'Course I am! Coming?"

"I'm watch on board tonight, Smithy; my turn tomorrow."

And it was just the same in the Ward Room where there was only one subject of conversation: shore-going. They drew lots for duty officer, because the repairs were going to take three days which meant four nights in harbour. The desire to go ashore had lain dormant for some time now.

"Buck up with the basin, Sub, you're not the only one who needs a shave!"

"Aha! Number One. You for the bright lights and sawdust too?"

Peter got a foothold in the washplace and started to lather his face.

"Me? Of course I am, you ass — get a move on or we'll be late for dinner."

"They keep open all night, they say. Where're we going anyway?"

"Captain's taking us — he's been here before. We're starting off in the Officers' Club anyway," Peter continued happily. It was grand to feel the cares of the world slipping from his shoulders.

"Poor old Pilot's got a raw deal," Taggart continued, "being duty tonight."

Peter wiped the soap from his face and stowed away his shaving things.

"His turn for a run tomorrow night, and then I'm duty the night after."

"It will be safe for me to go ashore then," Taggart chortled.

Peter caught him a flip with his towel.

"Come on, you look beautiful, Sub! Let's get cracking."

To be sauntering down the wide streets of Alexandria at dusk, lights twinkling from all sides before the blackout clamped down, was a heady sensation for men hungry to get ashore: it seemed like another world, dreamlike and unreal. By now Joe Croxton had joined them and these three, in slightly crumpled tropical rig, strode happily down the pavements until they found the Joint Services Officers' Club.

They found themselves in a society they had forgotten, a world of fast living, of artificialities, of impermanence. Peter smiled wryly to himself, for wasn't this the real world, the actual life in which one had to exist? And weren't the last six months, the period of the razor's edge, supposed to be the world of unreality?

A marble-tiled floor swept in a crescent before them, and across the imposing forecourt couples drifted, intent upon the business of forgetting. Death stalked not far away for, less than fifty miles to the westward, Rommel bided his time and remained poised for the attack, while these men with bronzed bodies, stale and exhausted from months in the desert, snatched twenty-four hours leave in Alex, the city with a Reputation.

The three submariners pushed open the swing doors. Down the opposite side of the long room there stretched a bar of incredible length, and, from behind this black, marble-topped edifice six barmen smoothly dispensed the multitude of orders, whilst long-bladed fans revolved idly overhead.

The officers chose a table by the open window at the far end of the bar, so that they could amuse themselves by watching the unaccustomed scene: the groups of men in quiet conversation, occasionally punctuated by raucous laughter, the rare officer and his girl who sought out the secluded corners of the room, the long-lost friends who had become suddenly reunited; they were all there, even to the noisy group which leant upon the bar halfway down, intent upon the rattling dice in the leather pot as they played 'liars'.

Joe bought the first round, which Ahmed, the nearest barman, deftly flipped upon the glass-topped table. They settled down comfortably in the cane chairs to enjoy the coolness, the peace of the evening and the golden glow of the sunset as it beat upon the white walls of the street outside, whence came the gabble of the crowds as they hurried home before the blackout.

It was delicious, no other word for it, as they sank deeper into their chairs and revelled in the contrast of the world of yesterday. In this luxurious ease, Peter had to pick up the evening paper to avoid falling asleep, and it was from this half-coma of forgetfulness that he first heard the altercation. He idly squinted over the top of the newspaper to see a Pilot Officer, obviously just in from the front line, arguing volubly with Ahmed who had become excited. Alongside the airman stood his companion, a Wing Commander, the dull red ribbon of a D.S.O. on his chest. He was huge, and even as he leant over the bar with his back to the crowd, you could see that he dwarfed most men.

The hum of conversation was much livelier now that the bar had filled with knots of carefree men and women, so that only a few heads turned momentarily to notice the argument. The younger officer had obviously drunk too much or he would not have been so abusive. Ahmed continued good-naturedly polishing the glasses behind the bar, but his dark eyes were beginning to smoulder.

"I tell you," the younger officer was shouting, "Wing Commander Barton gave you a pound. I saw him distinctly."

A wide grin beamed on Ahmed's face.

"No, sair, he gave me ten sheeling."

The Pilot Officer could stand it no longer. He gripped the lapel of Ahmed's coat.

"Give us the right change or I'll fix you."

Peter watched the inevitable incident with amusement; things were much the same in Alex as anywhere else! But now the gigantic Wing Commander had joined in and the bellow of his voice, mingled with the loud abuse of the Pilot Officer and Ahmed's high-pitched whine, had risen even above the general hubbub at the bar. Amused faces turned to watch the fracas, and shouts of encouragement wafted good-naturedly from somewhere at the back.

"Go on, Wingco, don't be seen off!"

The enormous figure kept his back to the crowd, but his eyes blazed angrily and his face flushed. He was obviously trying to play down the scene, a ridiculous argument in which he wanted no part. He hissed at his companion, who was, however, too angry to heed advice.

Peter's amusement was suddenly replaced by a heightened interest, as the Wing Commander tried to regain his self-control. The muscles in the giant's face worked convulsively, and then Peter noticed the man's hands. They were huge hams of hands and they hung at his side, the fingers flexing spasmodically. Then Peter's heart jumped, for something

129

happened which clicked the whole jigsaw into place. Something so insignificant that, if he had not seen it before, and, if it had not previously registered so indelibly upon his mind, would have passed unnoticed. He nudged Joe's knee beneath the table.

"Look, sir, look at that brute's knuckles."

Joe lowered his eyes.

"Good heavens, Number One, how horrible!"

The enormous hands were clenching and unclenching themselves with such force that the knuckles gleamed whitely, and, even above the hum of conversation, the crackling of the tendons was distinctly audible — a weird and unnatural sound.

"Don't stare, sir, please," Peter whispered as he peeped from behind his paper. "Look the other way and take no notice."

Suddenly there came a crash and a tinkling of broken glass as the Wingco pounded the bar with his fist. Cursing quietly to himself, he turned to pick up his cap, but as he did so, his eyes momentarily met Peter's from behind the top of the paper. There was a flash of recognition and then he slid quietly out by the side door.

Peter gasped; there was only one man in the world of whom he was scared, and it was the repulsive German officer who had trapped him at Castellare Poliano five months previously. He could never forget him, and even now he would awake in the night with hideous nightmares of this German. There could be no mistake — this was the man! Peter sat immobile watching the Pilot Officer put a brave face on it as he shook hands with Ahmed and then finished his whisky.

"Hullo, Johnny, what's all the fuss about?" asked another pilot who had forced his way through the crowd.

Peter couldn't hear the reply because they were soon on back-slapping terms and intent again on enjoying the evening.

"You look as if you've seen a ghost Number One. What's the trouble?" Peter heard Joe's voice from far away.

Peter slowly turned towards his Captain.

"I have, sir. Sub, order another round while the Captain and I go to the cloakroom, will you? And keep your eyes skinned on that Pilot Officer and don't let him go; we'll be back in a jiffy."

"Are you absolutely certain?" Joe asked in the privacy of the cloakroom, "certain beyond possible doubt?"

"Yes, I am, sir. There's only one person in the world whose knuckles crackle like that and that's Kramer, the S.S. Intelligence Agent who was in charge of the prison from which we rescued Harry Arkwright; sorry, I mean Lieutenant Arkwright, sir."

"Yes, but there could be lots of people who have this peculiarity under stress."

"But not also of his enormous size, sir. And there's another thing..."

"Yes?"

"He recognised me."

Joe whistled.

"Certain?"

"Positive. That's why he rushed out."

Joe paused and strode up and down the washplace for a full minute.

"I know that Alex is full of spies: we've all been warned about it, but what do we do now?"

"I reckon that we've got to act on this, sir. Kramer can't be here for nothing. As Captain 'S' told us, Kramer is one of Himmler's ace spies. Rommel wants to know when General Alexander is going to strike and where, so this information must be vital. What more natural than to employ a top-level spy to find out — Kramer, for instance?"

Joe slapped his thigh and made for the door.

"I'll go to the bar and get into conversation with the Pilot Officer. I'll ask his name and unit and give it to Intelligence. If it's genuine there can be no harm done. But if it's phoney…" Joe smiled, "anything might happen. In a few minutes, re-join the Sub and wait for me."

"Right, sir. Have a bet on it?"

"Yes. If you're right, you take the first week up in the rest camp, skiing at Beirut."

Peter grinned.

"Done, sir! I'll go and order my skis."

It was ten o'clock when they left the Officers' Club. Joe had engaged the pilot in conversation, and the officer had almost truculently supplied him with his name and unit. However, Joe had handled the affair tactfully, and was convinced that the pilot had no inkling of his purpose.

"You two get back to the boat, Number One. I'm going up to Army Headquarters. So long!"

"So long, sir. Don't be late."

Joe grinned.

"I'm going strictly on army business, Number One, don't forget that," and he chuckled as he disappeared into the darkness.

In the oppressive heat of the next morning, the incident of the night before seemed ludicrous, but Peter was soon engrossed in the day-to-day activity of seeing that the repairs were put in hand in the dockyard. Joe had gone ashore early in the forenoon and did not return for lunch.

Late evening found Peter alone in the muggy Ward Room and poring over the ship's drawings, and then he heard Joe's voice by his side.

"You've won your bet, Number One."

Peter stood up.

"Hullo, sir, was I right then?" and he grinned. "Me for the rest camp!"

Joe's face was grave as he slumped down on the settee and shoved his cap back from his head.

"You were absolutely right, Number One. But I'm sorry I can't honour my bet."

"Why, sir?" and Peter smiled foolishly.

Joe looked up at Peter and his eyes met his squarely.

"You've started something big, Number One. Intelligence have checked up on the Pilot Officer and he is bogus. They are shadowing him and already they have discovered that he is a spy who is transmitting from a secret transmitter. They're allowing him to continue sending signals while he is still unsuspicious and they have got the code. Counter-intelligence have been through to Malta and we've had an immediate recall to Lazaretto." Joe paused for a moment. "We sail at dark tonight," he said.

CHAPTER 13

The Vital Question

Like the sea, the sand is impartial, caring not for puny humanity and its struggles. The desert struck at both sides, and the soldier, like the sailor at sea, had to wrestle with it as well as with the enemy. The sun had passed its zenith and was beating down on the group of German vehicles concentrated in a circle some sixteen miles from the sea and five miles east of the desert oasis of Samalus. This was Rommel's Intelligence Headquarters, about ten miles behind the front lines, and it consisted of two mobile generators mounted upon vast six-wheel lorries, which fed the three transmitters that formed over half of the small encampment. The perimeter was completed by two caravans, a group of tents and an assortment of supply trucks. Camouflage netting was skilfully draped over the whole headquarters, so that it merged into the sandy landscape and became invisible to Allied reconnaissance aircraft.

The larger of the two caravans was the brain cell of the Intelligence Headquarters, while the other did duty as accommodation for the Officer Commanding of this nerve centre, General von Speidel, a spare man in his early fifties with a wiry frame like whipcord. He was tough, efficient and brilliant. Rommel had soon spotted the keen brain amongst his staff, and now von Speidel was engaged upon the one question the answer to which was vital to the Commander-in-Chief: upon which flank were the British going to attack? If Rommel knew the answer to this question, he could deploy and decide whether to attack himself before the British were ready, or whether to smash the enemy attack when it came on one of his own flanks — but which flank?

Von Speidel crouched over the maps in the larger of the two caravans. His steely eyes lifted an instant and flickered over the huge man who prowled like a caged beast across the restricted space of the caravan. Von Speidel felt slightly out of sorts, because he had offered the spare bunk in his caravan to his companion, and the huge man was not the best of colleagues under these circumstances. But he'd only had him since he'd arrived by U-boat from Alexandria and he didn't expect him to stay long. Von Speidel spoke sharply, an edge to his suave voice.

"Stop prowling about, Ulrich; you get on my nerves."

Kapitan Ulrich von Kramer stopped in his tracks and wiped the back of his bull neck with a sodden handkerchief for, in spite of the netting, the caravan was like an oven.

"I cannot get it out of my mind, *Herr General*; I am certain that the young English puppy in Alexandria recognised me," and he cursed under his breath.

Von Speidel put down his pencil. He had no time for temperamental spies but, he supposed, when a man like Kramer showed ill-temper, allowances had to be made. Himmler himself had transferred Kramer from some prisoner-of-war camp in Sicily; Castellare Poliano, wasn't it? Speidel took his time to light a thin cigar, his long fingers twirling the leaf, while he drew in the sweet aroma contentedly. But it now looked as if even the highly-rated Kramer had failed. Deliberately von Speidel spiralled a few smoke rings through his thin lips and his ice-blue eyes watched the circles bounce off the red-hot caravan roof one by one.

"Well, Ulrich, we have got to assume that all is well because our agent in Alexandria, Number…" and his mind trailed off as he searched for the spy's number.

"Number seven-o-one, *Herr General.* Herr Hammond, I call him," Kramer prompted. "He was Pilot Officer Hammond to the British," and he snorted disdainfully for he did not relish reporting the stupid incident in the bar to his superior.

Von Speidel's eyes flitted over Kramer: the man was a fool sometimes, but obviously out of his element, here in this blistering desert. He'd be far more useful in a cosmopolitan crowd, he could see that, with that extraordinarily mobile face which was so utterly featureless — a difficult face to place, to remember.

"We still can't give The Chief his answer, Herr von Kramer," von Speidel continued, "until we hear from your Pilot Officer … er…"

"Hammond. Pilot Officer Hammond."

"Er — Hammond, yes. Which flank are the British going to attack? Which flank, dammit, which?" and he threw his pencil on the maps while he stretched for his high-peaked cap. "Come on, Ulrich," he added kindly, "it's time for your Hammond's signal from Alexandria. I'm going to the Receiving Office to listen in; come along too, it might amuse you."

The glare outside hurt their eyes as they crossed over to the Wireless Receiving Office, even though the sun had passed its zenith. The shadows were already beginning to lean away from the trucks to make cool pools of shade wherein groups of off-watch operators lay spreadeagled.

The office was blistering with heat, and as von Speidel and Kramer leant over the operator, drops of perspiration trickled in runnels down their faces. The operator peered intently at the mesh-covered loudspeaker which he tapped gently with his right hand, while with his left he slowly swivelled the tuning knob. The hands of the clock had just passed five, and the spy's transmission was already overdue. Number 701 had always been punctual — ah! here he was now! The wireless operator slid a pair of earphones over his head, made his final tuning adjustments, and settled down with pencil and pad to take down the message. Von Speidel and Kramer watched the pencil slowly wavering across the buff signal-pad, while they listened to the slow Morse which pipped faintly from the loudspeaker.

The operator had been jotting down groups of figures for some minutes, when he suddenly stopped writing at the end of a group, his pencil still poised in mid-air. He looked up at his senior officer, glanced at the clock to complete the Time of Receipt, and then stood up to attention.

"Why did he break off so suddenly?" von Speidel snapped.

"I do not know, *Herr General*, but he was never a good operator," the man nervously replied. "He made a mess of his last signal."

"*Jawohl*, then get the signal decoded quickly and send it to me. It's important."

"*Ja, Herr General*," and the operator clicked his heels before handing the coded signal to a younger man, the office messenger, who immediately left the office for the Decoding Room.

Twelve minutes later the decoded signal from Alexandria was handed to von Speidel who was pacing up and down impatiently with Kramer.

"From 701," he read, "have vital information you require but suspect code possibly compromised. Will give you information personally. Request U-boat at rendezvous El Amiriya in seven days' time, next Friday, at two a.m. This is my last signal. *Heil Hitler.*"

Von Speidel glared at the signal and passed it to Kramer.

"What do you make of that?"

"*Donner und blitzen!*" Kramer swore. "I always thought Hammond a fool and now I know it. So we've got to wait over a week — I might as well return to my office in Matruh, *Herr General*, if you'll excuse me?" and Kramer clicked his heels to bow slightly from the waist.

"*Ja, Kapitan von Kramer, ja!*" the General replied, a shade too eagerly as he gave the Hitler salute, "I will keep in touch with you, and please keep me informed if you hear anything from your agents; anything, however small, do you understand?"

"*Jawohl, mein General.*"

"*Auf wiedersehen.*"

"*Auf wiedersehen, Herr General.*"

CHAPTER 14

Unlucky for Some

Agent 701 slammed the door of his top-floor flat behind him and clattered down the stone stairs. He was dressed in the uniform of a pilot officer in the Desert Tactical Air Force: khaki shorts and stockings, suede shoes, battered cap and khaki shirt upon which his wings were pinned. He halted on the pavement outside and idly glanced up and down the Alexandrian street while he casually lit a cigarette. Then, the picture of a young officer returning off leave, he started to stroll towards the shopping centre. He took a few steps, halted, and slowly turned about. Apart from a few Arabs passing on their daily business, there seemed to be no one following. His thoughts were racing, for this was the point of no return for him. Had he destroyed all possible evidence in the flat? Transmitter, batteries, codes — had he left anything behind? No point in returning now, hadn't he checked over and over again? He'd even burnt all his clothes, so that there could be no connection between 701 and Pilot Officer Hammond; he carried nothing with him except the folded daily paper which was tucked under his arm, his wallet which contained five pounds in notes and his crumpled identity card with the smiling face of young Pilot Officer Hammond. He took a long pull at his cigarette and resumed his walking to the city's crowded centre.

He had left his getaway to the last moment. It was four in the afternoon and he was on his way to re-join his unit forty-five miles to the west of Alexandria. He would take a taxi out to El

Amiriya, and then start walking along the coast road until he came abreast of the rendezvous with the U-boat.

He dimly remembered brushing through the crowded pavements, and staving off the gulli-gulli men. This was the last time he would see them, thank heavens! He had had enough of this stinking city with its evils and debauchery. For too long he had been living on his nerves, lonely and taut in a hostile society. But it had been worth it, and he had, he was sure, learnt the vital secret. The Eighth Army was going to attack on the Northern flank, all the signs pointed that way. He smiled to himself and started to hum the nostalgic notes of 'Lili Marlene'. Not long now — eleven hours and it would all be over — and who knows, he might even get the Iron Cross pinned on his breast for this?

"Look out, sir! Mind where you're going!"

There was a squeal of tyres, and he felt the mudguards of an Army jeep brush against his thigh. Two 'Redcaps' glared at him as the jeep jerked to a halt and then he saw the driver angrily throw in the gear lever and the truck bounced away down the street. He saw the white teeth of an Arab leering at him as he recovered himself, and he dusted his shorts before searching for a taxi.

I must be more careful, he thought. *If I go on daydreaming there won't be much left of me*, and, as he hailed the next ramshackle taxi, he found that his hands were trembling.

"Where to, sair?"

"El Amiriya, please, Johnny, and there's no need to hurry."

"Right, sair, right away," and before 701 knew what was happening the taxi careered madly down the street like a wild thing.

It was no use protesting, he knew from past experience, but an accident now would be disastrous. He shut his eyes and tried to relax back in the shadows of the seat, and then he gradually realised that the clatter of the traffic was dying away. His eyes opened and across the filthy coconut carpeting on the cab's floor there no longer criss-crossed the shadows of the motley world; instead, the sun spilled through unmolested and he looked out of the rattling window frame.

Ah, the sea! The beautiful blue of the Mediterranean, albeit somewhat muddied in the shadows, how beckoning and free it seemed! The demon at the steering wheel was singing his lungs out in the driving cab, and for the first time 701 felt a surge of happiness. Alexandria was behind him and only a disastrous misfortune could trap him now. He tapped on the separating window.

"Sair?"

"Drop me on the far side of El Amiriya, Johnny."

"Yes, sair."

"On the main road, and then I'll walk."

"Oh-kay, sair," and the demon tried to push the accelerator through the floorboards. They were soon through the little town, now a military outpost strictly controlled by Redcaps. 701 gave a pound to the grinning driver, who, in his delight, thought better of haggling. He'd never had a fare like this before!

With a sigh of relief, 701 watched the junkheap turn round and disappear up the shimmering road back to El Amiriya and Alex. There was nothing in sight, so he slipped unobtrusively off the main road and started walking northwards towards the minor road that ran parallel to the sea, two miles away.

The going was easy, and out here, by himself, he felt the load lifting from his spirit. A spring came into his stride, and he started whistling as he strode confidently down the narrow road which was not much wider than a cart track. To his right, the inshore marshes were gradually thinning out and, as his footsteps rang on the tarmac, flights of white seabirds lifted to hover above the reeds.

Dusk was falling when at last he spied his quest, a slight undulation on the foreshore, no more than a break in the coastline, but beyond the furthest pool of the inland marshes. His pace quickened and his pulse raced as he neared the rendezvous, barely two miles distant. He found himself whistling the 'Horst Wessel' and the treacly refrain beat time with his long strides.

"Want a lift?"

From out of the blue, the sudden question startled him from his reverie and his head jerked up to find a fifteen-hundred-weight truck purring beside him. At the wheel, a young gunner Captain leant forward to ask his question across the burly figure of a Sergeant whose arm was outside the door and whose hand was already fumbling with the handle.

"I'll jump in the back, sir," the Sergeant said helpfully.

701 was nonplussed. He hadn't thought of this embarrassing complication, because he had not known that this small road was used sometimes by the more perceptive soldiery. His thoughts raced desperately for a convincing answer to an everyday question. He looked away momentarily and when he turned again to face his questioners, his face was a mask.

"'Want a lift?' I said," the Captain asked impatiently. "I'm in a hurry — jump in!"

"No thanks."

The Sergeant and the Captain looked at him strangely and it was the Captain who spoke next.

"Wasn't that the 'Horst Wessel' you were whistling?"

For a split second 701 paused and then he saw that the hesitation had registered in the suspicious mind of the Captain.

Things were becoming awkward, *mein Gott!* Just when he had seemed so sure of escape, it was now or never with these two.

"Yes. What of it?"

The Captain looked at him long and curiously.

"It just seems odd, old chap, that's all: you've forty-odd miles to go and you don't want a lift!"

701 then did the one thing that an Englishman would understand. He blew up.

"What the heck has it got to do with you, might I ask?" the Pilot Officer exploded. "I'm waiting for a friend of mine to pick me up. Put that in your pipe and smoke it and mind your own blinking business!"

The Gunner grinned.

"All right, chum! Sorry, but you can't be too careful with all these spies about, can you?" and he shoved the gear lever home. "So long! Don't forget the Gunners when you're airborne!" and he jerked his hand in a farewell salute when the truck moved off. The familiar whine gradually grew fainter as the vehicle bumped its way westwards.

701 passed a hand over his sweating face, with fingers trembling from the ordeal.

"Phew! They were too suspicious," he muttered, and it was all he could do not to break into a run. He calmed himself and, making sure that the road was clear, he left it for the seashore as soon as he had passed the last of the swamps. With a huge sigh of relief, his head dipped below the dunes as his feet crunched on the grey shingle of the foreshore. He was now invisible from all these prying British, and, now that dusk was shutting down like a curtain upon another torrid day, the mantle of night would keep him safe until two a.m., when the U-boat should arrive.

But supposing she failed, or supposing that von Speidel and Kramer had never received his last signal? He could just imagine the submarine lying snugly alongside the jetty in Mersa Matruh, quite unaware of a lonely agent waiting with desperate urgency to be taken off. So many doubts assailed his highly-strung mind, that he decided to try and snatch some sleep. He moved to the protective proximity of the crumbling masonry which was all that was now left of the old lighthouse, disused since the middle of the nineteenth century. There was not much left of the original structure, but enough crumbling stonework remained to form a prominent landmark on this low-lying coast for those that knew where to look for it.

The old lighthouse was dark and silent now that night had fallen, and Number 701 remembered with a certain amount of regret the bed he had left behind him. The dark outline of the ancient city of Alexandria could still just be seen to the eastwards, and he smiled to himself when he looked at his watch. Eight-thirty — five and a half hours to wait!

He curled himself up in the lee of the tower, for the evening breeze was blowing from offshore, but he could not sleep, not only for the cold, but because his mind was in a tumult with the tension of waiting. If the U-boat failed to rendezvous at two a.m. what was he to do then? Better lie up here another day and try tomorrow night, rather than risk exposure again, but he would feel the pinch of hunger because he had deliberately brought nothing with him. Then, with his thoughts a-jumble, he fell fitfully asleep.

He sat up suddenly. How much time had elapsed? His watch showed one-thirty a.m. but had it stopped? He listened with relief to its steady ticking. Less than half an hour to go now and this ghastly business would be finished. He had worked hard and long under terrific stress, and he felt he deserved a break. He'd ask for leave from his arrogant Chief, von Kramer, but he didn't expect much change there, for that large bully was too good at the job himself and couldn't understand other people's weaknesses and wants. For instance, that behaviour of his in the bar of the Officers' Club was typical; nearly given him away it had — and now? Now it was five to two, and, with a joyous thumping of his heart, he stood up by the tower and looked to seaward. His eyes now were accustomed to the darkness so that he could pick out the sky above the horizon line.

Two a.m. His eyes were aching, so that he suffered a sudden shock when there appeared, right in front of him and barely five hundred yards away, the cascading and dripping silhouette of a large U-boat which had suddenly erupted from the sea. It was all he could do not to leap and shout for joy, as he watched a group of men assembling on the fore-casing. Then he heard a dull splash, and, as he strained his eyes he could just pick out a lean canoe lunging towards him. A few seconds later there was a scrunching on the beach and an overalled man leapt ashore.

From the darkness stepped Number 701, his heart singing as he advanced towards the dark figure.

"*Heil Hitler!*" he whispered.

"*Heil Hitler!*" the broad-shouldered man grunted as he offered the for'd seat to his companion. Then he pushed off from the shore, and his swinging paddles faded into the night whence they had come.

CHAPTER 15

False Colours

It is said that the British Secret Service is the best in the world. On this occasion, the Intelligence Headquarters in Alexandria had certainly lived up to its reputation. Acting swiftly and secretly upon the information received from the Captain of H.M. Submarine *Rugged*, it had made full use of the evening's carelessness.

Although Pilot Officer Hammond's sixth sense had warned him that something might have gone wrong after von Kramer had left him in the Officers' Club, he did not realise that his every movement was shadowed and faithfully reported; neither did he appreciate that his code had been broken, nor that his transmissions were being monitored.

In fact, when he made his last transmission asking for the U-boat to take him off at the El Amiriya rendezvous, he had asked for it in five days' time, not seven. His signal was jammed by the British so that the German Intelligence failed to receive it, but, at the same time his signal was acknowledged by the British, and not by the Germans. So Hammond was convinced that his signal had been received by the Germans and that the U-boat would be at the rendezvous in five days' time. He then destroyed his radio transmitter and all traces of his activities so that he would be prepared for his flight.

The day following his final signal, the false British transmitter again came on the air at Hammond's usual transmitting time. It was this signal that General von Speidel had received and he arranged for a U-boat to be at the rendezvous in seven days' time — not five.

The countermeasures had gone well in Malta also. *Rugged* had returned from Alexandria with all despatch and, on her first morning in harbour, Peter was surprised when he was called to a conference in Captain 'S's cabin. He found himself once again in that sparsely-furnished room, the scene of his agony four months ago when he had learnt of the tragedy of Harry Arkwright. It was a different atmosphere now, but nonetheless a solemn one as Captain 'S' began the proceedings.

"Gentlemen, we have stumbled upon a chance in a million," he began, "and we don't want to let it slip through our fingers."

He glanced at his audience, a small group of silent men. Joe Croxton, Captain of *Rugged*, Captain Jan Widdecombe, the Commando, and the First Lieutenant of *Rugged*, Peter Sinclair. They had all smiled when they first met, for the presence of Jan Widdecombe savoured of another cloak-and-dagger raid and Joe had groaned inwardly: if only they would leave him to his torpedoes! Peter grinned at Jan, the memories of their recent adventures welding an instinctive link between them, and then he heard the burly figure in the large chair unfolding the plan.

"You see, gentlemen, there is one piece of information which Rommel does not know and that is on which flank the Eighth Army is going to strike. He would sell his soul for that knowledge, and this is why his complicated espionage system has been built up in Alex and Cairo."

He went on to explain how false information had been relayed to the Germans on Hammond's frequency, and then Peter saw the eyes in the shaggy head begin to twinkle.

"Hammond, the spy, has asked for a U-boat to take him off in five days' time and that is why U-93 is sailing tonight. That is also why *Rugged*'s crew has been exercising in U-93 for the past two days and why her pendant numbers have been painted out and altered to U-679. It also explains why I have assembled you all here."

'S' relit his pipe before he continued to enlighten his somewhat apprehensive audience.

"You can speak German can't you, Sinclair?"

"Yes, sir: we lived there for a spell before the war."

"You can, I know, Widdecombe, and after your exploits with Sinclair ashore in Sicily, I thought that you two might like to team up again," and 'S' glanced at the two young men who were now grinning foolishly at one another.

"You see, we sent von Speidel a phoney signal — he's the German Big White Chief in Intelligence — asking for the U-boat in seven days' time. I have arranged for five of our Alex destroyers to meet the U-boat at the rendezvous...," 'S' paused before continuing.

"*Rugged*'s crew will man U-679 and will rendezvous in this position, one mile off El Amiriya at two a.m. in five days' time. A folboat will go in and bring off Hammond."

Peter and Jan were now tensed as they realised that they would soon be called upon to play their part.

"U-679 will then proceed to Mersa Matruh and surface off this German-held port on the same day that the U-boat is expected," and 'S' paused to search Jan's eyes before he continued. "The spy and his liaison officer from U-679 will then go ashore..." and 'S's voice trailed off into the silence. It was Jan who spoke first.

"We then contact the German von Speidel, sir, to plant the wrong information. Am I right?"

"Yes, dead right."

"… and then what, sir?"

"Come off by folboat the same night."

"Sounds easy, sir," Jan murmured, "but what is the wrong information?"

'S' paused.

"The wrong information is either the North or South flank," he said slowly. "This is so vital that I shall tell only one man, and he must report to me just before sailing tonight."

'S' watched the group and then he nodded at Jan.

"Yes, you, Captain Widdecombe," he said.

It was dark when U-679 slipped from her buoys, so dark that no one ashore could have sighted her slipping through the boom, and, in order to prevent any spy ashore being suspicious, she turned west before she dived. She then turned about, and half an hour later surfaced to set course for the rendezvous at El Amiriya, ten miles west of Alexandria. In the Ward Room, two men sat on opposite sides of the table, gabbling German at each other. The Captain of U-679 looked in and clicked his heels as they talked.

"*Heil Hitler!*" snapped Joe Croxton.

The two figures sprang up from the table.

"*Heil Hitler!*" they chorused, and then all three burst into laughter as they confronted each other with the ridiculous salutes. Jan gazed in admiration at the Captain's chest.

"*Mein Gott, Herr Kapitan,*" he exploded, "who to you gave the Iron Cross, *hein?*'

Joe twiddled the cardboard medal which dangled from his neck.

"The Stoker P.O.," he said.

CHAPTER 16

Mersa Matruh

U-679 had to kill time, two days to be precise, for it was upon perfect timing that the whole scheme depended. She went into the deep field to avoid any chance encounter with the enemy U-boat that was now steaming towards the Alexandrian rendezvous, and, thirty miles from the coast, she charged her batteries by night and went deep during the day.

It was five o'clock in the morning when Benson was handed a cypher to decode by the Petty Officer Telegraphist, Petty Officer James Haig, a Londoner born and bred.

"Immediate signal, sir," he said with a grin as he passed the Navigator a slip of pink paper — this was no time for deciphering signals.

But ten minutes later Benson reported to the Captain.

"Immediate from Malta, sir," he said, and smilingly handed the signal to Joe.

"Immediate. To H.M. Submarine U-679 from Captain 'S'," he read. "U-boat sunk by destroyers, no survivors. Carry out your instructions as ordered."

Joe smiled as he looked up.

"Poor devils," he said, "but at least it leaves the field clear for us."

Four hours later U-boat 679 was about to surface. Her jubilantly confident crew were an unusual ship's company for their speech was singularly un-Germanic.

"Proper skylark, ain't it, Bill?" demanded Ordinary Seaman Smith in the fore-ends.

Able Seaman Bill Hawkins smiled at he wiped the sleep from his weary eyes and slowly climbed to his feet.

"Not 'arf, it ain't, but it's too flippin' easy to be true, so far, mate."

Hawkins was serious for it was he who had brought off the spy that night from the rendezvous near Alex. He was tired with the strain and lack of sleep, for he had insisted on taking his part in the watchkeeping after the folboat had been stowed in the racks below.

"All part of the night's work, 'Swain," he had said.

The daylight bulbs had now been shipped, and Bill was curious to see clearly what his companion of the previous night looked like. The spy was sitting cross-legged under the fore-hatch, his bewildered eyes dull with the shock of bitter disappointment. How fooled he had been, and now he supposed there remained nothing but the firing squad.

Full of smouldering hate, he looked up at the burly seaman who now stood over him, a man of about five-foot eight, he would judge, but who carried an enormous barrel of a chest upon the lithe feet that moved like a professional boxer.

"What's your name, Heinie?" Bill Hawkins asked dispassionately, pity creeping upon him as he gazed upon the abject being.

"Hammond," the spy blurted, and then he checked himself, adding foolishly, 'you may only ask my name and number."

"Okay, Heinie, what's your number?" Bill grinned.

But it was no use. The spy had no more fight left in him, and, even as he turned away to blubber quietly in the corner, Hawkins could feel nothing but faint pity for him. It was difficult to believe that a creature like this could conceivably be directly responsible for the deaths of thousands of our men, and even alter the course of the war. Clad now only in a seaman's overalls, the cringing spy was nothing but a pitiful sight.

If the moment had not been so tense, the scene in the Control Room would have been farcical. Joe Croxton was the typical Prussian U-boat Kapitan: grey, belted overalls, an enormous pair of Zeiss binoculars slung about his neck, a closely-shaven head below a German Naval Officer's high-peaked cap. He was the perfect caricature of a ruthless Nazi U-boat Kapitan, as he strode arrogantly around the German Control Room.

"Are you ready, Jan?"

"*Ja, mein Kapitan*, I am ready," and Captain Jan Widdecombe smiled as he held out his hand, a day's growth of beard greying his finely-drawn face. With his piercing eyes and in Number 701's Pilot Officer's uniform of shorts and shirt, he looked not unlike the former spy who now lay whimpering in the fore-ends.

"All set, Number One?" grinned Joe.

"All set, sir," Peter replied sheepishly. In Malta, Captain 'S' had managed to procure an Unter-Leutnant's tropical uniform, and it was in this that Peter was now dressed: grey shirt and black tie, high-peaked cap, and with a Luger strapped around the waist of his long grey trousers, he would pass anywhere as a German naval liaison officer. Not that Rommel's men out in the blistering desert would know the subtle differences of uniform, because they regarded all those outside the Afrika Korps as beyond the pale anyway.

"Well, chaps, I'll surface now. I'll be here from eleven p.m. onwards, half a mile out, and Able Seaman Hawkins will be waiting for you with two folboats by that breakwater half a mile to the west of the town, which you all sighted through the periscope. Any questions?"

"If we run into trouble, will you be here tomorrow night?" Jan asked quietly. There was only one answer to failure or exposure — the traditional penalty meted out to spies which the Germans were not slow to award.

Joe looked long at Jan and Peter.

"Of course I will, if it's humanly possible. But I obviously cannot jeopardise my ship's company if we're hunted. If we're forced out, you had better try to make a rendezvous at the same time tomorrow night off Sidi Barrani."

"Yes, sir." Jan's eyes twinkled, for both knew that the alternative was futile: either they would have succeeded by nightfall or they would be dead by then.

"It's broad daylight up top, so boldness is our best chance," Joe went on. "German ensign all ready, Signalman?"

Goddard tapped the bundle of hessian under his arm.

"All ready, sir."

"All ready, Pilot?" Joe asked Benson who was the acting First Lieutenant now that Peter was otherwise engaged.

"Ready to surface, sir."

"Surface!"

"Surface, sir. Blow Main Ballast."

It took several minutes for Peter to become accustomed to the glare on the bridge, a brilliance reflected by the mirror-like surface of the sea which dazzled in this shimmering heat from the desert. He shielded his eyes with one hand and looked shorewards.

"Excuse me, sir."

Peter made way for Goddard who was trying to place the ensign staff in its socket, and then there was a gentle flapping as the offshore breeze spread the red and black flag, the ensign with its crooked cross. As Peter looked at the swastika streaming above his head, he squared his shoulders and felt his resolution harden within himself. He had been dreading this moment because he was going ashore as a spy — there was no other word for it. Disguised as a liaison officer, there could be no avoiding the fact that he was carrying out espionage. Until this moment, the whole episode had seemed impersonal and unreal, with no bearing upon himself — just another jaunt, in fact!

But now stark reality hit him squarely; it was too late to turn back and he hadn't the courage to refuse now. He felt his stomach heave as he began to realise what lay ahead of him for if they failed, and the odds were heavily loaded against success, Peter was looking his last upon his friends. He found his hands trembling as he longed to retract at this last moment, but as he looked at his Captain, he knew there was no going back now. With set face, Joe's piercing eyes glinted shorewards as they assimilated all details of the ramshackle port, picking out the few cranes working upon the small coasters, the jetties and installations, and then, slightly to the westwards, the breakwater which was the rendezvous for the folboat on this coming night.

"Launch coming over, sir."

Goddard's staccato report snapped some spring in Peter's subconsciousness, some overwhelming malaise that had been deadening his will to think. He looked at Jan leaning so confidently against the bridge-side, a picture of unruffled calm. But Jan was used to this sort of thing and was already completely living the part of a German. In his own mind he was already a German, and he thought and spoke as a German.

He turned towards Peter and the strong face was smiling as he asked in German, "Are you ready, *mein Herr*?"

"*Ja*, Hammond, let's go," Peter replied in perfect German and he looked at his Captain.

"*Auf wiedersehen, mein Kapitan.*"

Joe smiled.

"*Auf wiedersehen* to you too — see you tonight."

When the chugging of the launch became audible, Peter and Jan slipped over the bridge and down to the gun sponson where they waited, hanging over the rail by one hand and ready to drop into the launch as it drew alongside.

Apart from the signal lantern that started blinking from a blockhouse ashore, there was no other sign of interest in the waiting U-boat. Goddard kept replying with T's to its summons which seemed to keep the operator ashore happy.

Then came the coughing of the launch as the Arab coxswain went astern and Peter and Jan dropped neatly onto its bottom-boards. The Arab was gazing up apprehensively at the bridge when the Nazi captain nodded and pointed inshore. The dirty bowman hastily shoved off while the Coxswain wasted no time in getting clear of this sinister vessel that wallowed so sluggishly in the groundswell. As the boat turned stern-on, the two passengers clicked to attention, their right arms raised obliquely in salute to the Nazi who leaned nonchalantly over the bridge-side. No emotion cracked his face, but under his breath he was muttering quietly to himself. As soon as the launch disappeared around the pier at the entrance to the harbour, he turned slowly towards the voicepipe.

"Starboard twenty, steer North. Tell the First Lieutenant, Lieutenant Benson, that I shall be diving in five minutes' time."

He slowly straightened his angular frame and peered towards the conglomeration of white shacks that was Mersa Matruh.

Dust clouds whorled away to the east, while over the town two columns of black smoke spiralled. There was nothing to indicate the impending drama about to be played ashore.

As the launch chugged slowly up the harbour, Peter saw the hive of activity that seethed in the small port. There were small coasters unloading boxes of ammunition, tanks being swung out on rusty cranes, and petrol pulsating through the long hoses which jumped on the jetties. German sergeants prodded and bullied the Arab labour into frantic efforts at unloading and it was all too obvious that an all-out effort was afoot.

Peter felt a nudge from Jan. Right ahead was the landing stage, and standing thereon was a small group of soldiers, obviously the reception committee. Peter could not but admire Jan as he watched him from the corner of his eye; the picture of a highly-strung spy, he was eager to leap ashore to deliver his information as rapidly as possible. Peter's stomach sank as the drone of the engine faded and the launch turned a half-circle to swing alongside. This was his worst moment, for he did not yet know whether he was capable of carrying off a deception demanding such barefaced effrontery.

There was a bump and he found himself ashore, facing a young German officer in the Afrika Korps, his face a leathery bronze, his whole body a coiled spring of seasoned toughness from long exposure in the desert. He clicked his heels and saluted.

"Welcome to the Afrika Korps, *Leutnant*," he said as he gave the Hitler salute. He then extended his hand to Peter but self-consciously refrained from shaking Jan's.

Peter bowed from the waist, saluted and exchanged courtesies, his heart hammering in his ears as he listened to his own German.

"Thank you. We are glad to be here, I can tell you! This is Pilot Officer Hammond…" and he stepped forward to introduce 'the spy'.

Jan intentionally failed to meet the young officer's eye, but he held out his hand as he spoke excitedly.

"Yes, we're glad to be here, *mein Herr*! But where is General von Speidel? I have a message for him and it is urgent."

The soldier smiled and from his shirt pocket he produced a cigarette. He could see these two had been through something.

"Cigarette?"

"Thank you," Jan gratefully replied.

"Cigarette, *Leutnant*?"

Peter shook his head.

"No thank you, I do not smoke."

The German smiled.

"How wise you are! It's difficult to get these things these days because the British submarines sink most of the shipping."

Peter laughed. He was beginning to enjoy this.

"*Herr Kapitan*, let me introduce myself. My name is Krautz, Peter Krautz, and my Kapitan sent me to act as liaison officer for er — Pilot Officer Hammond here. What is your name?" Peter asked.

"Karl Koenig, *Leutnant*," and he bowed imperceptibly as he went on, "but we were expecting only one."

Peter laughed good-naturedly.

"Trust the staff to get it all wrong, Kapitan: we distinctly told them that a liaison officer would be accompanying Herr Hammond."

"*Herr Leutnant*," Jan broke in peevishly, "please address me correctly. I am known in the Secret Service in Germany as seven-o-one, and I would prefer to be called that now that I am amongst friends again."

"As you wish, *Herr...* seven-o-one."

Peter gave the Kapitan a wink and they both laughed.

"Shall we be going?" the German asked.

"Yes, please, *Herr Kapitan.* We are in a great hurry," Jan urged peevishly.

The Kapitan was irritated for he did not wish to waste his cigarette, and once they departed he would have to forgo it.

"If you insist..."

"I do insist, *Herr Kapitan.*" Jan's eyes were smouldering with impatience as he lived the part. "Take me to the General, please."

The soldier swore beneath his breath, pinched out the cigarette between his fingers, and carefully placed the stub in his breast pocket before running up the steps.

"Follow me."

Ten yards away, on the far side of a set of railway lines, there stood a truck by the side of which sprawled an enormous soldier, who sprang to attention as the Kapitan appeared. Beneath the peaked cap worn by all the Korps, his face was expressionless, but he too was a seasoned veteran of the desert. He opened the door of the cab and Peter was ushered inside.

"H.Q., Brandt."

"*Ja, mein Kapitan,*" and he ran round to his side and vaulted into the driver's seat while Jan and the Kapitan climbed into the rear.

During the drive to the Intelligence Headquarters, Peter remained silent and did not converse with the driver, as he felt it was the probable reaction of a German Naval officer towards a subordinate. He seemed to have judged correctly, for the driver remained mute as he impassively drove the fifteen-hundredweight truck through the suburbs and out into the desert. For a while they were held up on the coastal road by lines of transport struggling eastwards, tanks rumbling, six-wheeled trucks whining, 88mm guns on their mountings groaning and screeching; they were all there, moving up for the impending battle away to the east.

But then Brandt swung away to the south to leave the main road and the sea behind them. The sea, their only line of retreat — Peter watched it until it disappeared from view. In his mind he tried to memorise every mile of the journey, for they might have to find their way back at night, an ordeal he did not relish in this featureless desert, and he wondered whether Jan had brought a compass for he had forgotten to bring one. He looked at his watch: nine-thirty already, and then he saw the driver looking curiously at him. Had Peter made a mistake by keeping his English watch with its markings? Surely the soldier could not have seen it from there, in this bouncing truck?

"Nine-thirty," Peter volunteered.

The soldier grinned as he gripped the steering wheel with more concentration.

"We are late, *Herr Leutnant*," and the noise of the engine whined higher as he increased speed.

Peter sighed with relief, as he surreptitiously undid his watch and slipped it in his pocket. No experienced spy would make such an elementary mistake, and he smiled to himself as they clattered through a small Arab village. A German nameboard was driven into the sand at the entrance to this group of hovels. *Samalus*, he read. *Must be the name of this village*. But all the hovels seemed to be deserted now, and the only sign of life was a couple of soldiers sprawled out alongside a dump of petrol jerricans. They waved as the truck swirled by.

They were in the open desert now and the sun was right ahead as they motored down the sandy track, well beaten down by the coming-and-going of motor transport.

About due east of Samalus, Peter thought to himself, *and there are no landmarks now for miles around.*

On all sides the brown desert stretched out endlessly, rolling as far as the eye could see, a wicked wilderness of arid sand. It was the first time Peter had seen the Sahara and he did not like it. Then, far away in the distance ahead, he saw a small encampment of vehicles and he looked at the speedometer: four miles from the village, so the camp must be five miles from Samalus and due east of it. The driver pointed ahead and smiled. Peter grinned back, but his heart sank. So this was it, and the next hour would show whether the hare-brained scheme would work. The chances were that Jan and he would be dead within the hour if either of them made a false move; everything had gone according to plan so far, but so much could go wrong. Everything depended upon perfect timing now. Peter felt the muscles of his face hardening as his thoughts raced, but then his hand felt the Luger nestling so comfortingly by his side. *He and Jan would put up a fight anyway, but, for heaven's sake, Sinclair, pull yourself together, you're not dead yet, boy!* And he smiled to himself as the prospect of action beckoned, for the circular group of vehicles was only a hundred yards off now. A sentry came towards them but he lowered his gun as he recognised the driver and waved him in. As the truck came to a standstill in the sand, Peter saw a group of officers jump out from a square-shaped truck and come running towards them.

The liaison officer waited for the driver to open the door for him, and then he jumped out. Number 701 stood impatiently by the German Kapitan, and then all three approached the advancing officers. Peter dared not look at Jan, but concentrated on nothing but living his part as he sprang to attention.

"*Heil Hitler!* I have an officer to see General von Speidel."

A ferrety officer faced him, wisps of brown hair blowing from beneath his peaked cap. He was sweating profusely and his eyes were eager with anticipation as he hurriedly led them to the caravan which was set slightly apart from the trucks.

"*Heil Hitler!* Follow me, please, gentlemen."

From the corner of his eye Peter caught sight of faces peering inquisitively from behind trucks and from the windows of what appeared to be wireless offices, with their aerials bending in the breeze.

The ferret hustled them to the door and knocked.

"Enter!" a harsh voice rapped.

CHAPTER 17

The Dummy is Passed

For Jan and Peter the next few seconds stretched to eternity, a moment in time to be etched indelibly upon their minds, for they realised that their first impression would influence von Speidel irrevocably. One split second's doubt on his part about their integrity and the game would be up, for von Speidel had not become Rommel's Chief of Intelligence for nothing. A shrewd judge of character, he could smell out deception once his suspicions were aroused, so the few seconds that lay ahead were critical. All this flashed through their minds as they paused on the threshold.

Jan was magnificent as he acted the part of frustrated individuality, barging impetuously past Peter and forcing his way first into von Speidel's caravan.

"*Herr General!*"

Von Speidel stood in the middle of the small space, his hands behind his back, feet slightly apart as he quizzically gazed upon the agent who held the key to such vital information. The critical eyes bored through Jan, stripping him of all childish deceptions, peeling all superficialities from him. Jan met the searching eyes and held their gaze, knowing full well that if he wavered momentarily, the seed of suspicion would be sown. This duel of personalities cannot, in fact, have lasted more than five seconds, but they seemed to Peter the longest seconds he had ever known. To watch the two antagonists weighing each other up was like appraising a group of lifeless statues, they were so still. Peter held his breath — would those steely eyes of von Speidel's never leave Jan's face?

Then suddenly the General masked his eyes with drooping lids and, when he looked up an instant later, he moved quickly towards the spy. Jan held his ground and slowly proffered his hand.

"I am very pleased to see you, *Herr* … umm … Hammond, is it not?"

"Number seven-o-one, *Herr General.*"

Von Speidel chuckled quietly to himself, a gentle hiss passing through his thin lips.

"Ah, yes, seven-o-one," and he threw a protective arm round the shoulders of his important agent.

The spell was broken. Peter might not have been there, so engrossed were these men with each other, but it was all that he could do not to sigh audibly as he instinctively crumpled the peaked cap in his hand.

Then von Speidel, suddenly remembering the others, turned towards the ferrety officer.

"You may leave us, Seibricke."

Seibricke clicked his heels and the door snapped behind him, but not before disappointment had flickered in the greenish eyes.

"And who is this?" asked von Speidel when he appeared to notice Peter for the first time.

"I'm sorry, *Herr General,*" Jan apologised. "I forgot. This is Leutnant Krautz, whom the U-boat Kommandant gave me as liaison officer," he added condescendingly. "*Herr General,*" and Jan gestured theatrically, "permit me to introduce Leutnant Krautz."

Peter clicked his heels, bowed from the waist and saluted with outstretched arm.

"*Herr General*, I am honoured."

Von Speidel smiled: the Navy always affected polished manners.

"You better leave us while we talk, Leutnant Krautz," the General commanded as he nodded towards the door, but Peter paused momentarily.

"It is not necessary, *Herr General*," Jan cut in hurriedly, "Leutnant Krautz took me off from the rendezvous and knows all our secrets," and Jan laughed good-naturedly.

Peter felt von Speidel's eyes sweep slowly over him. It would be awkward if Jan and he were separated now, but Leutnant Krautz remained silent.

"You may stay, Leutnant, but this meeting is highly secret, you understand."

"*Ja, mein General*, I understand."

Peter swallowed when von Speidel turned towards the long table that ran under the long window.

"Come, now, seven-o-one," the General commanded. "Come and tell me what you have discovered."

Jan and the General leant over the maps. Jan's voice was noncommittal while he talked of troop movements from Alexandria and Cairo, of ammunition and stores, of railway departures and snatches of soldiers' conversations. His voice rose as he reached the climax of his report and turned to look directly at von Speidel.

"You see, *Herr General*, there can be no possible doubt: the Eighth Army will strike…"

"On General Rommel's right flank?"

"*Ja, mein General*, on our right flank," and Jan beamed broadly. The General was pleased, vastly pleased with his agent and he thumped him roundly on the back.

"*Das ist gut!* Well done, my friend, well done! I shall see that your efforts are fully recognised," and the intelligent face showed smiling appreciation. "But now I have much to do, so you must excuse me," he went on, "I must see the Commander-in-Chief and give him my appreciation," and he looked towards Peter.

"Leutnant Krautz," he commanded, "take Number seven-o-one back to my Security Headquarters in Matruh and report to my Deputy, the Officer Commanding Security. You will find the office off the main square, next to the Arab post office. I will telephone him and arrange for you to be escorted by the S.S. back to Benghazi where you will be returned to the Fatherland for some well-earned leave," and he laughed as he shook Jan by the hand. "I've no doubt you could do with some leave, eh, my boy?"

Jan smiled.

"Thank you, *Herr General*, I have tried to do my part. *Heil Hitler!*"

"*Heil Hitler!* General Rommel can now make his dispositions and deploy his forces, because your information does agree with my guesses," and he opened the door for his important agent — Seven-o-one had played his part in the jigsaw and now von Speidel had no further use for him.

As the door slammed behind them, they heard von Speidel getting through to the exchange.

"Get me the Deputy Chief," he was saying, "yes — and utmost priority!"

Accompanied by the impatient German Captain, Leutnant Krautz and the Agent travelled back to Mersa Matruh in the same truck. In the back, Jan was secretly hugging himself with delight, and it was difficult to hide his emotions from the ebullient Afrika Korps Kapitan.

"Cigarette?" the soldier asked above the clatter and jolting of the truck.

"Thank you, *Herr Kapitan*, I will."

"Your mission was successful?"

"Very."

The Kapitan soon gave up: these agents were a funny lot and were never communicative. They smoked in silence and Jan chuckled inwardly. So far, so good! They had sold the dummy and von Speidel had bought it completely. All that remained now was to get back safely on board U-679 without raising the alarm. It was now barely noon and eleven hours remained before they could rendezvous with the folboat off the breakwater. Eleven long hours! Somehow they must play for time before being sent off to Benghazi. At the worst, they could abscond from the transport arrangements, but that would be bound to arouse suspicion; anyway, another half hour would tell, but he wished he could have a word with Peter, sitting in the front seat there, with only this flapping canvas between them.

"Here we are, thank heavens!"

The truck swept across the dusty square and halted outside the one-storeyed white building labelled 'Poste'. They were escorted a few yards down a side street which adjoined the post office, and then the German Kapitan saluted and left them as he pushed open the door which led into a dark interior.

Across the white door a large notice proclaimed in black Teutonic capital letters, 'S.S. KOMMANDANT', and then underneath in smaller capitals, 'DEPUTY SECURITY CHIEF'.

Peter faltered, his hand brushing the Luger, as he looked at Jan's set face. To both of them had come a premonition of disaster, and both were unwilling to cross the threshold.

"After you, *meine Herren*," the silky voice of the soldier reminded them, "after you."

CHAPTER 18

Ill Met

"We wish to see the Kommandant."

Peter had preceded Jan and they had both been confronted by the dapper figure of a young S.S. officer, immaculately turned out with the usual S.S. smartness.

"Names?"

Jan spoke up deferentially.

"If you please, *Herr General* von Speidel telephoned about our transport to…"

"Names?" the officer rapped, "no one goes in to see the Kommandant without giving their names."

"I am agent Number Seven-o-one, and this is Leutnant Peter Krautz. We wish to see the Kommandant."

The man looked them over and then brushed past the steel-helmeted sentry who stood motionless by the door through which he disappeared. While they listened to the murmur of voices, Jan looked at Peter and raised his eyebrows imperceptibly. Peter slowly moved his hand to the Luger and Jan nodded.

"Leutnant Krautz!"

Peter jumped when he recognised his name and then he was ushered into the inner sanctum. He heard the door close behind him and then he found himself alone with the Kommandant who was standing by the window with his back to him.

He was a huge man — at least six feet four, Peter judged. An egg-shaped head jutted from a powerful neck which pivoted

168

from the most enormous barrel of a chest Peter had ever seen. The man appeared to take no notice of Peter, a bad-mannered habit for which he was renowned; to keep a suppliant waiting was one of the idiosyncrasies which he enjoyed, for it placed him where he belonged, far above normal mortals.

"Your name you say is Krautz, *hein?*" the voice asked caressingly, while the man still stared through the window.

Peter was nervous. Why should the Kommandant be suspicious of the name?

"*Ja, Herr Kommandant*, and General von Speidel said we should be sent on to Benghazi if you would arrange it."

The reply seemed to fan some flame of resentment in the Kommandant's soul for he became unreasonably agitated, a note of anger rising in his voice.

"I am in command here, Leutnant, and I never leave anything to chance."

The massive frame still sprawled against the window, and with horror Peter watched the ham-like hands with their stubby fingers picking off the flies that crawled up the wire mesh of the window and then squashing them deliberately. A little heap of dead insects splotched the floor at his feet. There was something in that broad back which disturbed Peter, some vague feeling recalling something he had perhaps dreamed in his subconscious sometime before. That broad back reminded him of something and he racked his brain for recollection.

"But, *Herr Kommandant*…"

"Don't 'but' me, you young puppy!" the man shouted. "Who do you think I am?" and in his anger he started to swear uncontrollably at the window. Then Peter noticed the man's hands: the fingers were flexing horribly, the tendons crackling over whitened knuckles. And then it was that something clicked in Peter's brain.

Yes, he was sure of it now! He had seen that huge frame twice before, once but recently in Alexandria. The first time had been under somewhat similar circumstances, months ago in Castellare Poliano, when von Kramer had been leaning against the window of the prison cell; *and that's why my skin prickles*, Peter thought. And now this horrible trick with his fingers had confirmed Peter's recognition.

It was Kramer all right, the ruthless S.S. Kommandant and agent whom he had recognised in Alex, and here they were again, about to meet face to face. When Kramer turned round, he was bound to identify Peter, after their recent mutual recognition in the club in Alexandria. Peter slipped off the safety-catch of his Luger.

Kramer spun round suddenly.

"You…"

Peter stood stock still, watching the pinpoints that flickered in Kramer's eyes for a sign of recognition, but mercifully anger blazed too fiercely for rational thought. Leutnant Krautz remained unrecognised.

"… do as I tell you, Leutnant."

"*Ja, Herr Commandant*, and Number Seven-o-one? Shall I escort him to Benghazi?"

Kramer paused to cast a contemptuous glance at Peter, and then he crossed to the window, pressing an electric push-button on his desk as he did so; but once again he spoke to the window, with his back to his visitor.

"Don't worry about Number Seven-o-one, Leutnant: I know him well — in fact, I only left him recently in Alexandria; we were working together and I reckon he can take care of himself."

The door clicked open.

"Ja, Herr Kommandant?"

"Send in Number Seven-o-one."

"Jawohl, Herr Kommandant."

Peter felt his heart banging against his ribs as the significance of Kramer's words sank into his mind. Seven-o-one and Kramer actually knew each other by sight, so the game was up now for Kramer would instantly recognise Jan as a fraud — it only needed a few seconds, then it would be all over. Peter's hand closed firmly on the handle of the Luger as he loosened it in its holster.

"What I cannot understand, Leutnant Krautz, is why your name does not appear in the Navy List — you did say Peter Krautz, P. Krautz, did you not?" the voice demanded silkily, the anger abating while he peered through the window at the blistering whiteness of the square outside.

The door clicked once more, but Kramer was too intent on emphasising his superiority for he kept his back to his visitors.

"Number Seven-o-one, *Herr Kommandant,*" the S.S. officer announced and the door shut hurriedly upon them; the S.S. man had heard the storm rumbling through the wall and he knew when to make himself scarce.

For a split second, Kramer remained with his back to them. Jan saw Peter draw the fingers of his left hand across his throat and then turn his thumb down, while with the other he snatched at the Luger and held it behind his back. Jan was puzzled but he slipped the Commando knife down his right sleeve so that the handle touched his curled fingers reassuringly. If it was to be a rough-house, he was ready...

The silky voice continued quietly at the window, while the stubby fingers continued to increase the toll of dead flies. "So you've arrived at last, have you, Hammond?" he said as he turned round slowly, "but you couldn't leave…" and then his words faltered as he saw the strange face staring at him.

"You're not Hammond," he gasped, and then the eyelids hooded the piercing eyes, as he sidled towards the bellpush on his desk. At last Jan understood, but in that split second the three players stood motionless while the truth dawned upon them.

Kramer's arm stretched for the electric button, but with his finger poised in mid-air he froze where he stood, as he looked down, mesmerised by the square snout of Peter's Luger.

"Don't move, Kramer!"

And then into the German's consciousness, it all came flooding back: the young puppy who had recognised him in the Officers' Club! Yes, that was it! The youth who had battled with him in Castellare Poliano! What infernal bad luck! They seemed fated to cross each other's paths, but he would have to go carefully now, for the young Englishman's hand was steady on the pistol and the eyes that watched him were merciless.

"Get over by the wall, away from the window!"

Kramer considered rushing them, but the gun was just out of reach and 'Hammond' had moved to the door. His eyes, too, were granite hard and were watching like a lynx. No, he would have to move cannily and bide his time for they hadn't a chance, and he backed slowly against the wall, his face now working in perfect self-control.

"So, gentlemen, you've won Round One, but how do you expect to get out of here alive?" the voice asked caressingly as it played for time.

Peter cut him short.

"Do exactly as I say, Kramer, or I will shoot you out of hand. Our chances are slim, but if you make one false move, we'll take you with us," and Kramer could see that the safety-

172

catch of the Luger was off. Looking at this Englishman, there was no doubting his words.

Jan's voice cut in crisply by the door.

"We'll have to take him with us, Peter — a dead Kommandant would give the whole show away. Kramer had better lead the way and we'll follow just behind."

"Where to?"

"The waterfront and the back streets where they won't be looking for us," Jan suggested. "We can hide down there."

Kramer's eyes were darting from one to the other, like a rattlesnake about to strike.

"Right, Jan," Peter snapped, and then he turned to Kramer. "Listen carefully, chum, and do exactly as I say, or else…" and he jerked his pistol. "I shall lead you out of this office, and, once outside, you are to turn round and give an order to arrange transport to Benghazi for us."

"Ready for midnight, tonight," Jan butted in.

Kramer nodded as he whispered, "*Ja*, I understand."

"And then," Peter went on, "you will turn back to me and state publicly that you are taking us on a tour of the town and the countryside and that we shall not be back until late. Got that?"

"*Ja.*"

"Well, now repeat what I've told you."

Kramer spoke swiftly, his face a mask of inscrutability.

"Right! Don't deviate, *Herr Kommandant*," Peter said, motioning Kramer towards the door with his Luger, "don't deviate one trifle. And now you will excuse me if I go first," and he slid to the door, as he slipped the Luger back into its holster.

"Ready, Jan?"

"Ready!"

Peter turned the door handle slowly, and as he did so he felt the heat of Kramer's breath gushing down his neck, while from the corner of his eye he could see Jan close behind. As the door opened, he saw the S.S. officer leap quickly to his feet at the far end of the room. About twenty feet, Peter reckoned, twenty endless feet — the slightest hint from Kramer during this next twenty feet and the whole plan would be jeopardised — Rommel warned that the information was false, U-679 compromised, Bill Hawkins in the folboat ... in this fraction of a second the hideous alternatives stretched before him. Twenty feet...

Peter raised his voice as he stepped boldly into the room.

"Thank you, *Herr Kommandant*," he said loudly, taking two long strides into the centre of the room and turning round quickly, "at what time shall we be here for our transport to Benghazi?"

For a moment Kramer paused while the world stood still, Peter and Jan fixing him intently with grim resolution. It was now or never for Kramer, a moment of decision, a moment for strength. It is odd how a man's mind works in moments of crisis, but instinctively, if there is a way out from paying the supreme penalty, he will discover it in his mind in nine cases out of ten; and Kramer's mind was not exceptional.

If I raise the alarm now, Kramer reasoned within himself in this interminable moment, *I shall expose the whole enemy plot, but lose my life*, and the future of his promising career gleamed before him. *But if I hold my tongue, I will find a way out later, when their guard has dropped*, and his darting gaze momentarily crossed the steel-grey pinpoints that were the pupils of Peter's eyes. Kramer had made his decision, and above the hammering of Peter's heart, he heard the German giving his orders in a normal voice.

"*Kapitan!*"

"*Jawohl, Herr Kommandant?*"

"These two officers are to be given road transport to Benghazi at midnight tonight."

"Midnight, *Herr Kommandant?*"

Peter had backed to the doorway, but now his heart stopped still and his hand crept across his thigh for the Luger, while he waited for Kramer's answer.

But Kramer let slip his second opportunity, as he again rationalised within himself.

"I said midnight."

"*Ja, ja, Herr Kommandant,*" the S.S. Kapitan replied hurriedly, "midnight."

Then Kramer moved to the doorway, barely six feet away, and Peter opened the door for him.

"By the way," Kramer nonchalantly threw over his shoulder, "I shall be taking my … er, friends with me for a tour of the town and the countryside, so don't expect me back in the office this evening," and the massive frame brushed past Peter and into the glare of the street outside. As Jan closed the door behind him, he saw the Kapitan shaking his head and heard him muttering to himself, "Unusual! The Boss is in a hospitable mood today!"

Peter blinked and shaded his eyes from the glare, as Jan closed up on the other side of the conspicuous figure of the enormous Kommandant who had now donned his desert cap.

"Thank you, *Herr Kommandant,*" Peter grinned as he felt the tension slipping from him, "and now take us straight down this main street to the east. Then turn left down to the waterfront when I tell you," and Peter pointed down the main thoroughfare that led eventually to Alexandria. If any suspicious eyes were watching, there could be no doubt as to which direction the incongruous trio were progressing. They strode down the middle of the street while groups of listless Arabs watched them from the dark corners.

"Nice town you've got here!" grinned Jan at his discomfited adversary.

Kramer grunted, his thoughts ceaselessly searching for a chance to turn the tables.

"Pretty dirty, though," Peter chipped in, "but it will be much better when the British get here!" and, if looks could kill, Kramer's glare certainly came near to it.

"Shall we go down here, *Herr Kommandant?*" Jan asked happily when they came to a small alleyway which led off from the main street and down towards the port. "I should love to see the waterfront!"

The Arab quarters were dark, and the nearer to the waterfront they walked, the more evil-smelling and sinister the hovels became. The Germans were not loved by the population and even Kramer was glad when a shaft of daylight dazzled them at the end of the alleyway; and then the dockyard road, pierced by rusty railway lines, crossed at right-angles.

"Stand still," Peter whispered suddenly.

Down the road marched four soldiers of the Afrika Korps, magnificent specimens of manhood, and Peter saw one of them nudge his companion as they recognised the uniform of the S.S. When they strode by they turned their heads smartly, their faces inscrutable as they saluted the dreaded S.S. Kramer hesitated, but then briskly returned the mark of respect.

Jan had been searching for a likely hideout and across the road a line of warehouses stood, looking directly over the harbour. At the right-hand end of this block jutted a two-storeyed lean-to with a small triangular attic.

"Keep in the alley, Peter, and follow when you hear me whistle," Jan said, and, when the road was deserted, he strolled over to the building, and then silently disappeared. A few minutes later Peter heard a low whistle coming through the slatted grille of the attic of the lean-to which was used for storing fishermen's nets.

"Cross over now," Peter whispered, and, as he strolled across, Kramer looked up and down the road hopefully. Peter followed closely and then they found a ramshackle ladder propped against the roof from whence another low whistle issued.

"Up you go!"

Kramer swore but clambered slowly up into the loft to disappear into the darkness above, Peter following closely on his heels.

"Perfect, Peter!" he heard Jan whispering from the gloom and from the all-pervading reek of tar which issued from the bundles of nets. "You can see the whole harbour from here, except to the westward which is screened by the outer breakwater."

Peter hauled up the ladder and looked around the netting-loft that now seemed like a cage with its wooden slatting that allowed for ventilation. Their eyes soon became accustomed to the darkness, and through the slats they had a perfect vantage point.

"Sit between us, please, *Herr Kommandant*," Peter said, "and then there can be no mistakes, can there?"

Kramer's huge bulk perched itself upon a coil of netting so that he had to bend his neck to avoid hitting his head on the corrugated roof, but he said nothing, as his eyes riveted upon something he had seen outside. Peter watched Kramer like a lynx. But then Kramer spoke softly.

"You haven't a chance, gentlemen — not if you came by submarine."

"Why not?" snapped Peter as Jan crawled to the slats. Then he turned towards Peter, and even against the light he could see Jan's face was deathly pale.

"Entering harbour, Peter," he croaked, "two destroyers! They're sliding past the breakwater now, and another has just let go her hook outside."

CHAPTER 19

Change of Plans

A cloud of despair descended upon the fugitives in the netting-loft, and as their despondency increased, so Kramer's attitude changed to one of servile co-operation.

"Well, my friends, what can I do for you, now that you cannot leave by sea?"

"You can shut that silly trap of yours and keep quiet," Jan snapped.

"It's a long walk home," Kramer leered.

"Listen, Kramer," Peter interrupted, "we aren't fussy whether you are alive or dead, but just at the moment it suits us to keep you alive," and as Kramer spat contemptuously, Peter continued, "Shut up, or we'll fix you."

The giant sprawled back on the heap of fishing nets and said no more, but he did not try to hide his amusement as he watched the two Englishmen crawl to the far side of the loft. They had been up here for three hours, but the heat was now diminishing gradually as Peter and Jan recast their plans in whispered undertones.

"Five-thirty, Peter."

"Three hours to go before twilight."

Jan grunted as he shifted his cramped body.

"Do you think Joe will risk sending in a folboat tonight?" he whispered.

"Shouldn't think so. That Wop destroyer is anchored too far out for him to risk it. Hawkins would have to pass round under her stern."

"But you know Hawkins…"

"Too risky, even for him," and Peter laughed shortly.

And so the scheming went on, punctuated by long spells of silence as they tried to put themselves in both the Germans' and U-679's quandary.

"I think that one of us had better go down to the rendezvous at dusk, Peter, just in case," Jan said. "Joe may send Hawkins in early."

"Right. I'll go!" Peter replied. "You're better at looking after that hulking lump than I am!"

Jan laughed.

"If we have to make the other rendezvous at Sidi Barrani tomorrow night, we'll have to spin a likely yarn to Kramer's H.Q. or they'll wonder where he's got to."

Peter nodded.

"Thank heavens you remembered that, Jan! We'll do that when I get back from the breakwater, shall we?"

"All right, but I reckon we could send a message if the Kommandant here will oblige," and Jan jerked a thumb towards the recumbent Kramer as he went on, "he can give it to one of his Afrika Korps boys to deliver to H.Q. in Matruh." Jan raised his voice, "Good idea, Kramer?" he asked.

The German's eyes glittered from his deep-set sockets.

"You'll get nothing out of me, you English pig-dogs," he snarled.

Jan snapped a notebook from the breast pocket of his pilot officer's shirt.

"Got a pen, Peter?"

Peter pulled a fountain pen from his pocket and handed it to the Kommandant.

"Write, Kramer, in your normal handwriting."

Kramer threw the pen back at Peter, and then, in a movement so swift that it went unnoticed, Jan slipped the point of his knife below the German's shoulders.

"I'll kill you now if you don't, you brutish lout," Jan whispered, a merciless flicker in his ice-cold eyes. "Do as I say!"

Kramer shot bolt upright as he read the resolution in the Commando's eyes, and then he held his hand out for the pen.

"What do you want me to write?"

Peter and Jan crouched on either side while Kramer scribbled their dictation in a curiously neat and pedantic handwriting.

Cancel my order for transport to Benghazi for the two Intelligence Officers. I am accompanying them myself in a staff car and will not be back until late tomorrow night. Kapitan Holst is to take charge of the office in my absence.

"Now sign it," Jan added quietly.

The pen slashed the paper with a vicious scrawl.

"… with your rank," Peter prompted.

When he had finished, Kramer sank back on the netting, while Jan carefully folded the message and replaced it in his notebook. Then he looked at Kramer.

"When we meet the right man, *Herr Kommandant*," Jan said quietly, "you will give this to him and tell him to deliver it to your Headquarters."

The sun was low on the horizon when Peter surreptitiously clambered down the ladder which they had left propped against the loft. He waited a brief moment while an Arab flitted by, and then he stepped on to the dockside road to walk briskly westwards towards the harbour and its central offices. He blessed the hive of activity that was Mersa Matruh, for even though it was now dusk, squads of men hurried briskly in all directions to unload the precious cargoes during darkness, while through the main dock gate there poured an endless stream of lorries whining into the night. The enemy were too busy to become interested in a lone Naval officer, incongruous though he was in this Afrika Korps town.

He quickly passed the gates and continued westwards, but it was difficult to catch a glimpse of the breakwater now, because the foreshore was masked by the usual bric-a-brac of sheds which litters all ports. Only once did he nearly come to grief when he remembered just in time to salute a fierce-looking Army officer who came pounding down the pavement from the opposite direction. Peter had to sidestep into the road to allow him to pass.

How un-English, he smiled to himself in the darkness, and then he caught sight of the glimmer of the fine of surf which was breaking on the low-lying foreshore. The buildings had now thinned out on his right, but to his left, an unbroken line of dark dwellings spread for another quarter of a mile.

An hour had already raced by when he slipped off the road to wend his way silently through the shacks which lined the foreshore.

Probably storerooms of some sort, thought Peter, *they're all boarded up and uninhabited.* The shadow of the breakwater was only twenty yards away now, whilst out to sea could just be seen the silhouette of the sleek destroyer swinging to her anchor.

Then suddenly, as he passed the deep shadow of the last two sheds, something smothered his face in a vicelike grip. He tried to yank at his pistol, but he was much too late as he tripped and fell softly to the ground. With all his might he struggled

182

and lashed out, but he was overpowered by the grip that remorselessly smothered him. He felt himself turned over like a child, and then the burly figure of an Afrika Korps soldier, his peak cap askew, sat squarely across his chest.

"I'm sorry, sir," a hoarse voice panted in English, "I didn't dare chance it."

The familiar voice of Bill Hawkins was music in Peter's pounding eardrums, and he stood up to shake himself as he felt the weight come off him.

"What a way to treat your First Lieutenant, Hawkins!" said Peter. "What's happened?"

They moved to the protection of the shadows between the sheds and then Hawkins unburdened himself.

"I'm afraid you'll have to put up with me again, sir!" Bill replied, and his grin gleamed in the darkness.

"What do you mean?"

"I've had to sink the folboat."

Good heavens, that's it, then! Peter groaned to himself. *No chance of escape now, nothing, nothing but* ... and then he snapped unreasonably at Hawkins.

"Why, for heaven's sake, why? That was our only chance!"

"It's all right, sir; the Captain told me to do it."

"Sorry, Bill," Peter apologised, the old familiarity of comradeship returning once more. "We've had a difficult time ourselves here, but it's good to have you with me again on a jaunt like this!"

"Proper skylark, sir, I enjoy it," and then Bill went on slowly as he remembered his wife and child whom the enemy had slaughtered. "Sort of gives me a chance to get my own back, if you know what I mean. I can't forget what's happened."

He pulled himself together and poured out his story.

"Captain said I was to give you this message, sir: 'Rendezvous Sidi Barrani tomorrow night at eleven'. You will have to find your own way off because there are no more folboats, and there are three of us anyway. Also he couldn't risk it with these 'ere destroyers!"

Peter smiled in the darkness. It was just like Bill not to mention his own exploit of slipping undetected past the anchored destroyer. Yes, it was good to have Bill again, even though their number was becoming somewhat large. He looked at his watch: nine-thirty. "Come on, Bill," he muttered, "two hours will have gone before I get back," and then he looked at Bill in amazement as the stocky seaman stepped out of the shadows, the perfect impersonation of the Afrika Korps. "How did you get that uniform?"

"Borrowed it, sir," and the teeth gleamed.

"Where?"

"Ashore, sir."

"Who from?"

"Don't rightly know his name, sir, but he was a German pongo."

Peter chuckled as they hurried back through the shadows.

I wonder what Jan's been up to, he thought. *I've been far too long.*

They reached the lean-to without incident, Hawkins following fifty yards behind Peter, because he did not dare increase the distance for fear of becoming involved with any loquacious Germans. Bill sighed with relief when he eventually rejoined his First Lieutenant who was waiting by a ladder.

"What's that, sir?"

Peter followed Bill's gaze. On the top rung of the ladder was pinned a note in Jan's handwriting:

Sorry! I've had to clear out as we were disturbed by this unbidden guest who was hiding stolen German loot — a very laudable pastime nevertheless! I will send off transport-signal, but, until we meet at rendezvous S.B., I remain,
Yours, in company with Little Fritz,
Jan

"I knew it," Peter cursed. "I felt that something had gone wrong. Let's nip up top."

As he groped in the darkness of the loft, his hand touched something soft and hot, and when he increased the pressure there was a muffled groan.

"Pull up the ladder, Jack," Peter whispered, "we're inboard," and Bill chuckled in the restricted space as he closed the lattice door upon them.

"Do you think this is a trap, Bill?"

"How do you mean, sir?"

"Do you think that the Huns wrote that note, having captured Captain Widdecombe, and are just waiting to pick us up?"

Bill scratched his head.

"In that case we'd better scarper, sir."

"But I think it's genuine."

"Why, sir?"

"It's the way Jan would express himself, and no Hun could imitate it."

"You're right there, sir, but supposing someone comes to look for him over there?" and Bill nodded towards the trussed Arab whose eyes gleamed in terror from the gloom.

"I don't think they'd come here for him, Bill, for he was hiding loot and would be bound to choose somewhere unknown to anyone else. Let's stay here to get some sleep before tomorrow."

"Right," Bill replied, holding out a bar of chocolate, "would you like some 'nutty', sir?"

Peter's hand closed over the chocolate and he mumbled his gratitude as his palate relished the food.

"It's bound to be pretty hectic tomorrow, sir. We'd better get cracking early if we're to make Sidi Barrani by nightfall; it's about eighty miles, ain't it?"

"That's about it, Bill, but let's take tricks at sleeping while the other guards the prisoner, and we'll be up and away at dawn."

"Right, sir. I make it ten-fifteen so I'll watch for the first two hours and then give you a shake. You go ahead and have a good sleep," and he chuckled ominously, "you never know what tomorrow will bring."

But Peter, an exhausted man, whose last thought was whether he would live to see another sunset, had already slipped into the half-world that precedes sleep.

CHAPTER 20

Dance and Skylark

The dull red glow from the open fore-hatch dimmed and went out.

Joe breathed a sigh of relief as he felt the distant tremor of the hatch when it shut. He was surprised at the speed of the report which came up the voicepipe, "Fore-hatch shut, sir," but then he remembered that these German hatches were shut by handwheels and not by samson bars.

"Clear the bridge, stand by to dive."

He automatically went over to shut the voicepipe cock, and as he did so he had his last look at Mersa Matruh by night. Even though he was trimmed right down so that only the conning tower was now visible above the surface, he had not dared to take U-679 any closer to that awkward destroyer which was anchored just off the pier, because detection would probably mean failure of the counter-plot and the death of his friends.

Able Seaman Hawkins was a good hand, by heavens, he was! Without a murmur he had quietly shoved off in the folboat and disappeared into the night, to give the silhouette of the destroyer a wide berth. Everything depended upon that man and his message, but perhaps Sinclair and Widdecombe were dead by now anyway — and now he had deliberately sent Hawkins after them on what might be another tragedy. But so far there had been no reaction from the destroyer whose silhouette showed up so clearly, and there was hope if only the two men ashore could contact Hawkins.

"Dive, dive, dive!"

U-679 went deep to draw away from the land, and, after surfacing ten miles offshore, she trundled slowly westwards on her main engines to get in a good charge.

Joe was feeling happier when he prepared to dive the boat at dawn. Perhaps it was the beauty of the cold first-light behind the thick cloud that caused his soul to respond, or perhaps it was because of an undisturbed night, but whatever the reason he felt relaxed, and almost elated, so much so that that sixth sense of premonition which comes to all seamen was dulled momentarily: he never heard the lone Wellington that had been shadowing him on trailing engines. How was the pilot to know that U-679 was British-manned, as he swooped from out of the clouds to let go his stick of four bombs?

It was all over in less than six seconds. The bridge personnel flattened themselves on the deck, for Joe had not even time to reach the Klaxon push before the third bomb crashed alongside, only twenty feet clear of the port quarter, and then the Wellington pulled out and away on their port bow to disappear into the trailing cloud.

"Straddled all right!" Joe shouted through the fine spray that showered upon them from the near miss, "but no direct hit, thank God!" and he steadied himself from the violent roll caused by the explosion. He searched for the klaxon push once again, but as his fingers found the knob an urgent voice bellowed up the voicepipe.

"Captain, sir? Chief speaking."

"Yes, Chief?"

"Water's pouring in through the port exhaust manifold: I think the valve seating has been lifted by the explosion."

"How serious?"

"We daren't dive, sir."

Joe paused. His mind took in the golden dawn that was now breaking fast to the eastwards as the night clouds rolled away — a sure sign of another cloudless day.

"How long to repair, Chief?"

"Difficult to say, sir, but I think it will mean stripping down the valve-box. Can you cock her stern out of the water for me, as I can't work on it under water?"

"All right, Chief. Let me know how long you think you'll be as soon as you can."

"Aye, aye, sir," the Chief acknowledged calmly. Apart from the gentle swish-swish of the water lapping along the casing as she lay stopped and wallowing in the swell, there was an uncanny silence which contrasted strangely with the holocaust of the last few moments. How quickly the tables could be turned in war — one moment and all was going swimmingly, and the next, disaster — it took a few moments for human comprehension to grasp the magnitude of the catastrophe.

"Blow after main ballast!"

"Blow after main ballast, sir," a voice repeated hollowly up the voicepipe, and then, quite suddenly, the after-ends tilted sharply from the sea, the water cascading down the streaming hull.

"Blow for'd main ballast!"

"Blow for'd main ballast, sir."

Joe brought her to full buoyancy, and there she wallowed in a most ungainly posture, bows down and tail up, but at least her stern was well clear of the water, so that even the screws were visible.

Another day had burst upon them before the Chief climbed to the bridge to make his report, but his eyes were grave as they met those of his Captain.

"The repairs will take at least six hours, sir."

"Six hours?" Joe asked incredulously, as he looked at his watch — five forty-five.

"Yes, sir, although I don't think there's a fracture. If it's possible to dismantle the whole valve-box, I reckon I can do it in six hours."

The Captain paused and then he took the Chief to one side of the bridge, out of earshot from the others.

"I'm blinkin' sorry, sir," the Chief murmured, "but even working flat out at it myself, I don't see how we can do it in less time."

"Of course, Chief. But do you realise that if I had been on my toes, this might never have happened?"

The Chief paused, an older man than his Captain by ten years.

"If you'll excuse me, sir, that's nonsense."

Joe smiled wanly, a note of despair in his voice as he replied almost brokenly, "We're close to the enemy beach, we can't dive, we're surrounded by the Luftwaffe, and we've got to be off Sidi Barrani tonight to take off the shore party — not an encouraging prospect, Chief." Then suddenly Joe squared his shoulders as he faced the older man. "Well, we're not done yet, we're still afloat and I'm darned if these Huns are going to see us off," and then, the dark eyes smouldering with determination and the light of battle once again, he leant over the voicepipe.

"Ask the Navigating Officer and the Coxswain to come on the bridge, please." The Captain had regained his composure by the time that he had his senior men around him.

"Well," he began, "you see the sort of potmess we're in?" and he nodded towards the shore.

Benson and the Coxswain nodded, realising the gravity of the situation — no submariner likes remaining on the surface, a sitting duck for allcomers, friend and foe alike. Joe was watching the grizzled Coxswain, the backbone of the ship, friend and counsellor to all men, respected and almost reverenced by all on board. Slowly the parchment face turned towards him and an impish light flickered for a moment in the wise eyes.

"Permission for hands to bathe, sir?"

Joe did not find this amusing and his question crackled angrily.

"What do you mean, Coxswain?"

"Well sir, we can't dive, and if we stay on the surface out here we'll either be bombed by the R.A.F. or the Luftwaffe, because both of 'em reckon a submarine is fair game. Am I right, sir?"

"Right, Cox'n."

"Well, sir, I was just thinkin', if one of 'em could be persuaded that we were friendly, at least that would increase our chances by half."

"… and, after all, we are already a German U-boat, sir," Benson interrupted, "so it shouldn't be too hard to convince the Hun."

"Suppose we went close inshore, right by the beach, sir," the Chief chipped in excitedly, "to get Luftwaffe fighter cover. At least we should have two chances."

"Whereas now we have only one, you mean?" Joe asked as the possibility dawned upon him.

"Yes, sir," the Coxswain replied, "and if we sent the hands to bathe close inshore, the Hun couldn't possibly think that we were British," and his eyes twinkled again.

"By heavens, Coxswain, you've got it!" Joe said excitedly. "What speed can you give me on the starboard engine, Chief?"

"Full, sir."

"That ought to give us about ten knots, then, so we should be inshore within the hour."

Benson broke in quietly.

"Won't the Hun become suspicious, sir? I mean, they should know the whereabouts of their own U-boats."

"Right, Pilot, but isn't it quite possible that we are the boat that has returned from Alex with the spy?"

The Chief whistled.

"Of course, sir, so it is! Truth is always stranger than fiction, they say."

Joe was smiling once again, his drawn face deeply lined as he made his decision.

"All right, then, are you all agreed, for it's a life or death decision, you know?"

The Coxswain spoke for them all.

"We'll get by, sir," he said quietly. "Shall I tell the hands?"

"Go ahead, Coxswain, and now we have a little deception to do — Signalman!"

"Sir?"

"Hoist the Nazi ensign."

"Aye, aye, sir!"

"Pilot!"

"Sir?"

"Have two swastikas painted on either side of the bridge while we steam shorewards."

Benson was already halfway down the hatch, and, as he looked up, his young face was smiling.

"Aye, aye, sir!" he grinned.

It took longer than Joe estimated to reach the coast; firstly, because U-679 only made eight knots on one engine with her peculiar trim, and secondly because he decided to make for a point ten miles west of Matruh. It was just as well, because air activity was much less here; it also gave more time for painting in the black swastikas upon their white ground and for the Chief to prepare his party fully for the immense task which faced it.

Joe cast his mind back to the last attack he had made on a U-boat off Sicily, when he had missed her because she was so close and inside his turning circle. The picture of the bare-chested Germans, sunning themselves and singing on the bridge like charioteers off to battle, had always remained in his mind, and now he made full use of the memory.

"Coxswain on the voicepipe!"

Joe had settled down to a continuous day's watch-keeping on the bridge, and now, after half an hour's steaming, he could just pick up the low-lying coast of Cyrenaica.

"Coxswain on the voicepipe, sir," the brass pipe boomed distantly.

"Cox'n, send up six of the most sunburnt men, and tell them to be bare-chested."

"Have we any sunburnt hands, sir?"

"I don't know, but they have got to be by the time they get up here! Send them up quickly."

The coughing of the throaty exhaust from the starboard engine interrupted his thoughts — dismal and cheerless broodings of despair. They hadn't a chance, he knew, not a chance by all the rules of war: a quick and merciful chatter of machine-gun fire or the sight of approaching destroyers would at least put an end to this tomfoolery. But then he remembered Jan and his First Lieutenant, abandoned in that sandy desert, whose only hope of survival was the existence of U-679. And then Joe realised suddenly, with a clear shaft of reasoning, that the only way to survive was to almost overplay the part of a German U-boat. The more tomfoolery there was, the less possible chance was there of being recognised as British, and then he realised with a smile that, paradoxically, there was now more danger from a lurking submarine of the Fighting Tenth or from a wing of Beaufighters than there was from the enemy.

"Permission for six bare-chested hands on the bridge, sir?" a humorist boomed up the voicepipe.

"Yes," Joe snapped, and then murmured to himself, "if we must play the giddy-ass, then I suppose the Hun might as well have jam on both sides."

Then there emerged through the upper lid six of the most suntanned specimens that would not have disgraced even Monte Carlo. They stood before their Captain grinning shamelessly.

"Well, Smith, I never knew I had such a healthy lot in my ship's company!"

Smith grinned and his teeth gleamed white in the bronzed face.

"The Navigator lent the 'Swain his brown boot polish, sir."

As Joe roared with laughter, the tension eased for a moment and he gave them their orders.

"Sit astride the bridge rail and sun yourselves, lads, and don't forget, sing your heads off as if you enjoyed it. You never know who's watching."

And so the crazy bluff went on; by ten o'clock, U-679 wallowed half a mile off the beach, ten miles from Mersa Matruh, and in only five fathoms of water where she could not possibly dive. As soon as she stopped, Joe again trimmed her by the stern, and the Chief waded into his work, while from below there rang the unaccustomed ring of hammer blows.

"All hands to bathe, repeat *all* hands to bathe, Coxswain, with the exception of the Engine Room crew," Joe ordered. "Take it in watches so that we have continuous bathing until the Chief has finished."

"Aye, aye, sir, and shall I rig lifelines?"

"Yes, please."

Joe just could not believe that the scene was real, as he watched what might have been a leisurely peacetime occasion. "Hands to bathe!" he kept on muttering to himself. "They'll never believe this in Lazaretto, never!"

Down both sides of the submarine splashed the nude figures of sailors, shouting and skylarking for all they were worth as they revelled in the blue-green waters of the shallows. Less than three-quarters of a mile from the beach ran the coastal road, ribbon-like as it stretched across the desert. Even without his glasses, Joe could see truckloads of Afrika Korps soldiers yelling and waving with their caps.

"Blue Watch, hands to bathe!"

The incredible order reverberated up the voicepipe and another pink motley pattered helter-skelter along the casing to splash into the ultramarine sea, even before the first watch had left the water.

"Permission for the Chief E.R.A. on the bridge."

"Yes."

The Chief arrived on the bridge, his face dripping with perspiration which he continually mopped with his sweat-rag.

"How goes it, Chief?"

"Better than we could have hoped for, sir. The valve was unseated but there are no fractures."

"Thank God, Chief, and how much longer, d'you think?"

"Well, sir, we're just…" and his voice faltered as his eyes concentrated on something to seaward on the starboard quarter. "Hullo! What's this?"

Joe switched round and his heart jumped. Six black specks that grew larger with every moment spiralled straight towards them from out of the sky.

"Messerschmitts!" he whispered to himself, for he dared not instil panic if the bluff was to succeed.

Then he leapt on to the bridge rail, steadied himself against the standard with one hand, and with the other snatched off his Nazi cap to wave it uproariously above his head.

"Come on, lads!" he yelled, "wave to the blighters, wave for all you're worth!" and his arm swung frenziedly.

The sailors were not slow to catch on, as from the water they saw their Captain greeting the diving fighters. Then the bathers hove themselves upright in the water, laughing and waving with tremendous verve.

Joe glanced at the ensign which mercifully was fluttering nicely in the slight breeze. He could do no more now than watch with horror the yellow-snouted Messerschmitts screaming upon them in their final run-in.

"Oh God!" he whispered to himself. "What a shambles it will be if they open fire!" and he could not shut out from his imagination the ghastly picture of the packed swimmers in the water.

The leader was now fifty yards away and pointing straight at the bridge. Joe watched the leading edge of the wings, waiting to see the cannon's first spurt of flame, as the fighters tore into the attack. His heart seemed to stop and he felt himself swaying with dizziness as he hung by the standard.

And then she was over, flaps shuddering and engine chattering hoarsely, away in a graceful swoop towards the coast, to be followed by five more diving lunatics.

"Phew!" Joe grinned to the Chief who stood below him, still mopping at his forehead, "not much different from the R.A.F., are they?"

The Captain jumped down, waving to his men in the water, and then there came to him the sweet sound of men's exulting cheers in answer, so that he had to turn away for emotion.

"As I was saying, sir, before I was interrupted," the Chief went on, "I reckon it won't take as long as I feared — maybe another two hours."

Joe was silent for a moment.

"Good old Chief! That's fine: please do all you can because I can't stand much more of this sort of warfare!"

"Aye, aye, sir. I think I'll go below now, it's quieter in my Engine Room, if you know what I mean!"

The Luftwaffe episode had given them all confidence, for if they had fooled the aircraft they must surely be safe? But, nevertheless, when the Engine Room reported at a quarter-to-three that the repairs were completed, there was little delay in clearing the water of bathers.

By three-thirty the port engine coughed into life and when the black smoke had wafted away downwind, the manifold was tested and found to be satisfactory.

"Wish we could have brought off the shore party, sir," Benson said quietly as he stood by his Captain. "We're so close they could have swum off."

The submarine righted her trim and slowly turned towards the sea, while the bridge personnel waved heartily to the bystanders on the beach.

"So do I, Pilot," Joe replied, "but even with the cheek of old Nick, the impossible takes a little longer."

As U-679 quickly gained sea room, Joe slowly pulled the hatch over him while the water mercifully closed over them as she dived.

"Surely nothing else can stop us from making the rendezvous tonight?" he asked out loud. "Surely nothing can?"

CHAPTER 21

Disaster

It was not long after dawn had broken that the S.S. Kommandant of Security, Mersa Matruh, stepped into the middle of the road from the sandy verge that spread to the horizon in limitless desert. For such an elite corps, he was strangely unshaven and dishevelled, and his face bore the signs of strain, blue half-circles of weariness pouching beneath his deep-set eyes. His companion, a fair-haired dwarf in comparison, stood just behind him as he halted the green west-bound jeep that came whining down the road, its driver still half asleep at this early hour. But, Kramer was glad to note, the driver who was so cleanly shaven and smartly turned out belonged to the S.S. detachment under von Speidel's command. Here was a chance for a getaway from this self-assured Englishman, but he had to be careful. If he could remain unrecognised by the driver, so much the better, as the Englishman might be lulled into a false sense of security.

"Where are you bound?"

"Benghazi, *mein Kapitan*."

In the slight pause that followed, the driver noticed the smaller man close up behind the Kapitan.

"*Das ist gut!* We'll come with you as far as…"

Once more the driver was aware of a slight hesitation in the huge officer's speech, and at the same time he found it odd to note that his companion wore the hated uniform of a British Pilot.

"*Jawohl, mein Kapitan*, but what about the English officer?"

Jan cut in immediately, a laugh escaping from his open mouth.

"*Herr Kommandant*, explain to the driver who I am!"

Kramer swore bitterly beneath his breath as he felt the point of the knife pricking above his rump; this was a joke which he did not relish.

The driver had jumped out when he heard his superior addressed as Kommandant. Of course! This was the big bully they'd heard about — the chap in charge at Mersa Matruh. He clicked his heels and saluted.

"This is a friend of mine," Kramer said quietly. "We are on a job and we want to get to Sidi Barrani."

"Of course, *Herr Kommandant*, I understand," and the soldier smiled.

Jan stepped forward and thumped the man jocularly on the back.

"That's right, my friend. Mum's the word, of course," and he winked. Delighted to be treated on such familiar terms, the soldier jumped into the driving seat, and indicated the empty seat alongside.

"Thank you, my friend, but we shall sit in the back," and Jan politely motioned the Kommandant to precede him to the rear seats. Then suddenly they were off, bumping and jigging westwards down the deserted road, the cool wind of the early morning whistling about their heads, so that speech was fortunately impossible because of the clattering of the vehicle.

Sitting immediately behind the driver, Jan could watch Kramer sprawled over the mudguard casing opposite him. The man seemed to have lost all will to resist, in fact had become extremely co-operative. *They're all the same*, thought Jan to himself, *once they're licked they just curl up and whine*, and he looked at this pink-necked giant in disgust. The man's huge hands hung down on either side of him, the stubby fingers jerking from the uneven motion of the jeep and Jan shuddered. He looked away over the tailboard to the cloud of dust which the truck was kicking up and which curled away into the distance.

Already the deep orange of first light had changed to the piercing whiteness of early dawn, and this vast space of limitless desert was terrifying in its immensity. It was difficult to realise that two vast armies now lay facing each other just below the eastern horizon, preparing for the battle that would lock them in mortal embrace, one of them to rise no more.

"Cigarette?"

Suddenly Jan realised that his attention had wandered from his prisoner, for the man was holding out a packet of battered cigarettes towards him. Jan shivered as he saw the fingers, so thick and strong with their hidden power, fingers capable of squeezing the life out of him if given the chance.

Jan shook his head and smiled.

"*Nein, Herr Kommandant*, but you carry on."

He was almost sorry for the German, he suddenly realised. Poor devil! The brute's career was finished now, and how the man would hate having his leg pulled by his brother officers! Jan smiled; he'd never met anyone with so much puffed-up pride.

The jeep trundled onwards, putting mile after mile between them and Mersa Matruh, and each mile that flashed by was one more nearer to freedom and success. About eighty miles, Peter had said, eighty miles to Sidi Barrani, the new rendezvous with U-679; Jan wondered whether they would have better luck this time. *Better had*, he thought ruefully, *or I shall be the 'late' Captain Widdecombe*, and then his head slumped for a moment as the desire for sleep overcame him. When he awoke, he jerked suddenly to consciousness, his heart thumping with terror —

for how long had he dropped off? Then he realised that it could have been but for an instant, for Kramer was slumped opposite, apathy in the dulled eyes. Then Jan lifted his heavy lids from his blurred eyes and focused upon his adversary. Kramer's deep-set eyeballs were slowly curtained by his rubbery eyelids as they unfolded like a hawk's.

I must watch myself, Jan's exhausted mind clamoured, *watch, watch myself,* and he found himself muttering to the tempo of the jolting jeep, "watch myself, watch myself … watch myself."

Then, as his head jolted forwards, his eyes rolled upward in their last moment of sensibility. Suddenly he was warned, finally and irrevocably, for, from behind Kramer's hooded eyes he glimpsed two pinpoints of hate; sheer, unadulterated hate, flickering three feet from him, like the evil which burns coldly in the eyes of a poised cobra. Then he saw the hands hanging, tensed and crooked.

Jan sat up, jerked into alertness by this last warning — one more lapse and he was doomed, he was certain. Then the implication of his narrow escape dawned with all its horrible reality; another second and he would have dozed off, and nothing could have stopped those talons that swung so closely by him. From there it would have been easy, for Kramer had merely to drive back to Mersa Matruh and then only God knew what their fates would be, Peter's, the submarine's, his, and yes, perhaps even those of thousands of Britons now marching up to the front lines. Jan shivered, now fully awake — a near shave!

He felt the jeep gradually slowing down, and he looked out as a nameboard flashed by — 'SANYET EL MAMURA', he read, and then underneath in smaller letters, 'S.B. 43km, M.M. 80km'.

The bronzed face of the driver hailed them from the front seat.

"Gasoline, *Herr Kommandant*."

They all leapt out when the truck slid to a halt. The driver approached the couple of guards who were munching their midday meal by the pile of jerricans which formed the dump just outside the whitewashed village. The senior of the two men saw Kramer and they jumped to their feet. The elder helped the driver whilst the other went to deal with an east-bound fifteen-hundredweight that had just drawn in.

"Cigarette, Pilot Officer Hammond?" Kramer asked, adding sarcastically, "I'm sure you'll join me."

"Isn't it rather unwise near that dump?" Jan asked. "Better move over here if you want to smoke," and they moved towards the fifteen-hundredweight on the roadway.

"D'you mind if I give these lads a smoke?" Kramer asked.

"Not at all, go ahead," Jan replied, "the poor beggars are going through the same hell as we are."

They both strolled over to the group by the new arrival, and Kramer beckoned them to approach him across the road.

"Care for a cigarette?"

The faces of the two soldiers radiated pleasure and astonishment. An S.S. Kommandant so familiar? But war in the desert altered all values, and how they knew it!

"*Danke schön, Herr Kapitan*," they chorused as he held out the packet towards them.

"Light?"

"*Danke schön*," and Kramer struck a match for the guard.

"Light?" Kramer asked the driver of the fifteen-hundredweight.

"*Danke schön, Herr Kapitan*."

As the match flared, Jan looked up at the driver of the jeep who was striding towards them; simultaneously, the new arrival bent low over Kramer's cupped hands to light his cigarette while Kramer, his back to Jan, crouched low to help him. In that instant, Kramer seized his chance.

"Don't look up," he hissed, "and listen carefully, soldier. I am in deadly danger and this man with me is a spy," and then he cursed loudly as he pinched out the match, "*Gott in Himmel! Another light?*"

The flame flared once more and Kramer bent low over the drooping head which waited for a light, so that Jan could not possibly hear.

"Warn S.S. H.Q. in Mersa Matruh: I am being held hostage and the other two officers are spies. Tell General von Speidel. Understand?"

The crouched soldier dragged at his cigarette, stood up and took a long pull while he looked hard at Kramer.

"*Das ist gut, mein Kapitan, das ist gut — danke schön,*" and he shook Kramer's hand warmly in gratitude, at the same time giving a slight nod of his head which did not go unnoticed by Jan who glanced rapidly at Kramer. But the hooded eyes betrayed nothing, and then the soldier turned away and clambered into his truck.

Did Kramer pass a message? Jan wondered, *but even if he has, I can't blow out his brains here and take on these other two as well.* His hand slid to the small automatic strapped inside his shirt.

The fifteen-hundredweight swung out from the depot, and, as it revved past them the driver shouted, a leer gloating upon his secretive face, "*Auf wiedersehen, Herr Kommandant!*" and the words floated mockingly after him as he pulled away at full speed.

Jan was now certain! The look on the man's face and the address of 'Kommandant' both denoted that he had been tipped off by Kramer. So that was the way the wind blew and he'd better get moving!

"Get cracking, Kramer," Jan whispered crisply, "into the jeep!" and he nodded towards the refuelled truck.

"No hurry, my friend, is there?" Kramer taunted, "we've plenty of time," and he strolled nonchalantly towards the vehicle. In an hour and a half's time at the most, the whole Afrika Korps would be alerted, even if he, von Kramer, lay stiff and cold. "No hurry, I am prepared to wait!" he whispered to himself.

Jan was desperate while he waited impatiently for the driver to start.

"Hurry, driver," he snapped, "the Kommandant is joking, for we have an appointment in Sidi Barrani at three o'clock," and he laughed good-naturedly as he sat down opposite Kramer.

The jeep bumped into motion and quickly left the depot behind, then on through the raggedy hamlet and out into the desert beyond, the kilometre posts flashing by all too slowly.

Jan concealed from Kramer that he knew of the message now being borne eastwards, and he merely watched him coldly across the jeep. The Englishman now knew where he and his friends stood and he groaned within himself. Due to his one moment of carelessness, the whole plan would be exposed in an hour or so, and the chances for Peter would be nil. And the submarine? Jan groaned again, but when he looked at those devilish eyes glittering so close to him, a spurt of anger kindled within him. He had not trained for in-fighting for nothing, and he knew just how to hit a man without killing him. In the jolting jeep, he gently slipped off the safety catch of his automatic and waited his opportunity.

As he gazed over the tailboard at the whirling road behind, from the corner of his eye he watched Kramer turn his head in the same direction. Then suddenly Jan struck with his right hand, a lightning rabbit-punch just above the first vertebra. The stiff neck slackened and the head rolled forward as the hulking body slumped forward unconscious. Jan moved swiftly to the same side as the crumpled man, and, as the weight distribution shifted, the jeep lurched wildly to warn the driver that something was amiss. He looked back quickly, but the bulk of Jan's body shielded the damning evidence. He leant forwards, grinning as he gazed up the road and waved to the driver. The soldier was reassured and Jan went swiftly to work, trussing up Kramer with the tow rope that lay coiled on top of the toolbox.

He waited for a clear road and, slipping his knife down into his right hand, he crouched poised behind the driver; then he tapped him on the shoulder.

"Stop here, please."

The jeep slowed down, the driver leant forward to apply the brake, and then the world whirled about him in a myriad stars as a heavy blow struck him at the base of the neck.

As Jan leapt over the tailboard, the driver's foot settled on the accelerator to send the engine whining into a crazy crescendo.

"Blast!" Jan shouted to himself, and he yanked the slumped body from the seat before the engine thrashed itself to pieces. He quickly dragged the man across the road to a small dune twenty yards away, and then, stripping the man's shirt into shreds he bound and gagged him.

"I can't murder the poor fellow," he panted, "even though I don't like Huns," and he loped back to the jeep which was now ticking over gently. As a car hurtled past him from the westwards, he waved happily, and then he turned back to the crumpled body of Kramer lying on the floorboards. Yes he was alive all right, he decided when he rolled back the eyelids; and then, to make doubly sure of retaining Kramer, he whipped off the man's trousers and threw them on to the front seat, at the same time checking his bonds and frisking him for hidden weapons.

He looked at his watch: a quarter to one. How time had flown! He jumped into the driving seat and put his foot hard down as he whipped into top gear.

"About twenty miles to go," he groaned out loud. "Five hours till dark, so I'll have to lie up."

Then a black cloud of misery engulfed him, so that he barely noticed the road bouncing ahead of him.

"What's happened to Peter?" he whispered as he remembered the messenger driving eastwards. "I've betrayed him. Oh God! He hasn't a chance now."

CHAPTER 22

The Net Closes

There was no need for Hawkins to shake Peter, for at five-thirty, just as the first light of dawn was showing sombrely through the lattice, the shock waves of four explosions rumbled distantly from seawards.

"What was that?" Peter asked, wide awake.

"Sounds like a stick of bombs, sir — well out to seaward," Bill's voice answered wearily, "probably our old boat!"

"Just the bombing of another aircraft, I suppose, but the Captain's too fly to be caught by that!" and they both laughed, as a grunting from the shadows reminded them of their Arabian companion.

"Mornin', Johnny!" Bill grunted cheerily, "had a comfortable night?"

"Don't be an ass, Bill, let's get going before the port livens up."

Peter cautiously opened the slatted door. The waterfront was deserted, so they slid the ladder to the ground and left the protesting Arab, taking care to leave the door open so that he would be found eventually. Two shadows flitted into the street, then, squaring their shoulders, they strode out into the wakening world, their footsteps ringing loudly on the cobbles.

"We don't sound like two guilty men, sir!" Bill whispered.

"We'll be out of here soon," Peter replied, as he lengthened his strides. They were across the dock entrance and the cobbles changed to a dirt road which wound through the back streets. They met no one, for this was the quarter which was out of bounds to the troops, squalid and ramshackle in its poverty. Then out on to the main Sidi Barrani highway, a metalled motor road for a few miles, but eventually deteriorating to the usual hardpacked sandtrack. They walked south-west for an hour and a half and, apart from one truck which passed them going westwards, the road was deserted.

They were becoming anxious about their direction, but then, in the distance, the road curved to the right, and as they rounded the bend they saw a stopped truck pulled up by the side of the road, the driver stretched out beneath the rear axle. As they drew nearer, the man crawled out and wiped his hands upon an oily rag.

"Are you thinkin' wot I'm thinkin', sir?" Bill whispered, looking at Peter.

Peter nodded.

"I'll talk and you nobble him, Bill."

"Aye, aye, sir — it'll be a pleasure."

They reached the German as he was climbing back into his cab.

"Good morning," Peter greeted the driver, "having trouble?"

While Peter went up to him on the left-hand side of the truck, Bill casually walked to the opposite side.

The driver leant out, looked at Peter curiously, and then spoke respectfully.

"*Jawohl, mein Leutnant*, I've had a bad oil leak," he explained, "but I've tightened the…"

He said no more as a huge hand clapped itself around his face, while another arm encircled his throat with a bear-like hug. Peter did not draw his gun, it was so easy; he merely left it to Bill who trussed the man up like a frightened fowl. Bill then walked off the crossroads with the dangling body slung across his shoulders and dumped it four hundred yards away behind some scrub.

"He'll be all right, silly beggar," Bill grinned, "until the sun gets high."

"Thank you, Able Seaman Hawkins. Would you care for a lift to Sidi Barrani?" Peter asked gravely.

"Thank you very much, sir, I wouldn't mind at all!" and then the starter whirred, the gear was thrown in and the truck lurched off on its trek westwards.

It was wonderful to be on the move, careering wildly down the track which led them kilometre by kilometre away from the hated Mersa Matruh. Peter kept his foot hard down and the revs hummed happily in a high-pitched scream, an enchanting melody to their unmusical ears.

"Only about ninety kilometres to go before Sidi Barrani," Peter sang out as another distance-post flashed by.

"But I shan't believe it till we get there," Bill yelled back, "it's too good to be true, sir. Hullo! What's that?" and he peered seawards.

The road was now only two miles from the coast, and the low-lying shore was easily visible from the driver's seat. Well in, barely half a mile from the thin line of surf, the familiar outline of a German U-boat appeared to be at anchor, her Nazi ensign flapping lazily in the slight breeze.

"Well, blow me down!" Bill expostulated, "the Huns have got a nerve!"

Peter chuckled as he saw the distant white splashes of bathers in the water.

"Nothing so pleasant ever happened in *Rugged*, did it, Hawkins?"

"No, sir, never. Pity the Captain isn't around, for he'd soon slip a fish into them!"

But then an explanation flashed through Peter's mind and he was thoughtful for some time as the possible disaster became apparent to him.

"It may not be so funny, Bill. She may be the Hun which was supposed to have brought off the spy at Alex."

"Crippin, sir, you mean…"

"Yes. If she is that submarine, the destroyers must have missed her and by now our whole deception scheme has been blown wide open."

"Blimey! Then the whole Afrika Korps might be out looking for us?" and Bill gave a long whistle.

"Quite probably, Bill; we'd better get a move on. I only hope that Captain Widdecombe is well ahead of us by now and lying up in Sidi Barrani."

With the engine roaring deafeningly, the two men sat in silence while the sun curved high into the sky to render the cab unbearably hot. After another three quarters of an hour, the engine seemed to lose power, in spite of Peter's foot which was nearly forcing the accelerator through the floorboards.

"Blast it, Bill! There's something wrong with this engine. Look, the radiator's boiling!"

Wisps of steam were spurting through the radiator cap in a fine spray, and then slowly the engine grunted to a halt as Peter regretfully slipped in the clutch.

"Well, Bill, the old girl has brought us sixty kilometres anyway."

"That's better than a slap in the eye with a wet haddock, sir — and certainly better than on my flat feet," and then he continued ruefully, "What's to do now, sir?"

Peter scratched his head thoughtfully.

"Well, Bill, we've got to get a truck somehow — there's no other way of reaching there by tonight."

"Except by camel, sir."

"Fortunately I can't see any."

Bill rubbed his unshaven chin and made a tentative suggestion.

"We could ambush the next truck that comes along, sir."

"I've got it, Bill," Peter chipped in, "there's nowhere for us to hide, so we'll have to stage a breakdown which blocks the road and forces an oncoming truck to halt."

"Right, sir," Bill grinned, "here we go," and they started to push the vehicle across the road.

"Quick, Bill, how are we going to get a wheel off?"

"Won't a puncture do, sir?" and Bill held out the blue-tempered blade of his Commando knife.

"No, we'll have to do better than that. They all have punctures at one time or another and they wouldn't stop; besides, we ought to push it off the road, if it were a puncture."

Bill had already jumped into the back, where he rummaged about until he found a jack and brace.

"Here we are, sir; front or back?"

"Front: it will look more dramatic," he said as he yanked the steering wheel over. "She'll cant well over with the wheels like this," and in less than four minutes the left front wheel was removed and sent spinning off the road.

"Quick, Bill, there's something coming down the road from the west, about a mile away."

"I'm going to enjoy this, sir," Bill leered as he yanked at the jack while he stood well clear. There was a splendid *crash!* and the truck lurched over to lean drunkenly to the left.

"Get under and pretend to have a look, Bill," Peter snapped as he tossed the jack into the back. "We mustn't fail, or we've had it; leave the talking to me."

Bill jumped under the sagging vehicle and slid upon his back until his face was under the engine: from here he could watch Peter's progress, but he was only just in time for he could already feel the pounding of the vibration upon his back from the approaching truck which seemed to be travelling fast.

Peter placed himself between the ramshackle wreck and the oncomer, loosening his Luger as he did so. He raised his left hand and waved it excitedly as the truck careered madly down upon them.

"Heck, Bill! There's a madman driving."

Then there was a squealing of rubber tyres as the driver leaned angrily out of the cab. He seemed truculent and in a hurry.

"What's wrong?" he shouted, "I'm on an emergency and can't stop."

"Sorry, soldier, but we're stranded," Peter apologised. "Give us a hand to right this van and then you can be on your way."

But the driver paid no heed to Peter as he glanced at the pair of legs that stretched from under the breakdown. The trousers had ruckled upwards and above the left boot a black sock showed. But across the top, upon a large white name-tab, the name plainly announced — HAWKINS, W., A.B.

"*Hol's der teufel!* You must be the two escaped spies!" the driver expostulated with a sharp intake of breath, his eyes sweeping across Peter to play over his uniform.

When Peter saw the startled eyes gazing in suspicion at him, he drew his Luger and pointed it at the man's chest.

"You're right. Get out."

But the driver was a brave man, and, even as Bill scrambled out from beneath the broken-down lorry, he threw in his gear lever, accelerated, and started to swerve to his left, straight at the Naval Leutnant.

Peter jumped in the nick of time, and, as the cab door swirled past him, he fired. The poor devil never had a chance…

Then, with a dead man slumped over the wheel, the truck started to career madly in a tight circle, with ever-increasing speed as the body's weight fell upon the accelerator. Peter leapt on to the running-board of the cab, yanked open the door and, while the vehicle swayed crazily, he pushed the shapeless hulk across to the far side of the cab.

"Phew!" he panted as the truck came to a halt, "that was a near shave!"

Bill came up panting.

"You all right, sir?" and then he saw the body. "Poor devil! He had plenty of guts," and then he added breathlessly, "there's another truck coming, sir. You'd better get out and do the talking while I deal with this."

But as Peter leapt out, he could see there was no time to dispose of the dead man. The truck was now well off the road, so there was room for this east-bound lorry to pass by. But, as he sauntered breathlessly towards the highway, it was clear that this was a six-wheeler, fully laden with troops bound for the front line; from the sides, he could see them bristling with firearms. His heart sank: it had to be pure bluff this time for they couldn't take on a whole platoon, and as he stood waiting by the roadside, he felt his hands trembling from the shock of having killed a man in cold blood.

The whine of the six-wheeler decreased as it slowed to a crawl and then the driver leaned out of his cab.

"What's up, *Herr Leutnant*? Want any help?"

Then, as Peter watched the soldiers leaning over the side in curiosity, he heard his own voice; it was from far away and curiously detached.

"It's all right, thank you. We've come across an abandoned truck, but there's nothing we can do — you carry on!"

Peter saw that Bill was sprawled across the open side of the driving cab, but mercifully nothing strange was showing. Some of the soldiers, however, were trying to bandy words with this silent soldier who would not reply. Peter groaned within himself, his mind racing.

"Good luck!" he said to the driver, "better get on your way."

"Oh, that's all right, Leutnant," the humorous-faced driver retorted, "they're in no hurry to be cannon-fodder," and he jerked his head towards the men in the back.

Heavens, thought Peter, *they're going to act the Good Samaritan*, and he backed away as the driver jumped out, shouting, "Come on, lads, let's get this wreck off the road!"

The troops needed no encouragement as they leapt helter-skelter over the tailboard. They stretched themselves and looked in amusement at the ramshackle van in the middle of the road.

"Well, Korporal," Peter said, "we'll be off — thank you for stopping."

"Sergeant, sir, please," the man replied, looking curiously at Peter, "just a minute, Leutnant…

But Peter strode quickly towards the waiting Bill, waving as he went. The purring engine responded and the truck leapt forward, but through the mirror he saw the soldiers running to the breakdown lorry, pause, and then rush back to their six-wheeler. Then, instead of proceeding on its way eastwards, he just caught a glimpse of the monster backing and turning to follow them.

"At least we've got a start, Bill," he shouted, "and we're faster than they are. But they are too blessed suspicious."

"Roll on, Sidi Barrani, sir! We seem to have stirred up a hornets' nest."

Peter glanced in the mirror: the lorry was still out of sight and now their engine was going superbly, but they had over thirty kilometres to go before reaching the port.

"Get that poor chap's clothes off him, Bill. When you're ready, take over the wheel while I change into them."

Ten minutes later, the body was bundled over the tailboard and on to the kerb, and then Bill took over the driving while Peter donned the soldier's uniform.

"Ugh!" he grunted in disgust as he felt the warm stickiness of the collar. "I hope this dries off before we get there," and he wiped his hands on the trousers before scrambling back to the seat beside the driver.

"How far to go, Bill?"

"Twenty-five kilometres, sir."

Peter looked at his watch: twelve-thirty. How time had flown! But the sun had now passed its zenith, and there were still eight hours to sunset.

"We'd better ditch this truck and lie up on the outskirts of the town, Bill," he shouted above the roar of the engine. Peter grinned as he watched his stalwart comrade, face set, enormous hands clutching the wheel in happy abandonment to the thrill of speed. It had been a lucky day for him when he rescued Bill on that dreadful night in the English Channel.

Half an hour later, the outskirts of Sidi Barrani showed on the horizon, and they hurriedly changed places.

"No sign of the six-wheeler, sir."

"No, thank heavens, but we haven't much time. Let's make for the desert side of the town."

"They won't expect us to go that way, sir."

"That's what I am hoping," and as a small road led off sharply to the left, Peter swung the wheel over. The street soon deteriorated and he had to reduce speed for the potholes before they sighted a likely cul-de-sac. Then, to the astonishment of a frightened Arab woman, he switched off the engine and they both leapt out, leaving the abandoned vehicle where it stood.

"Come on, Bill, keep your eyes skinned for a likely hideaway where we can lie up till dusk."

"Aye, aye, sir, but I hope this ain't going to be another busted flush."

They were to know seven hours later.

CHAPTER 23

A Matter of Inches

"Sounding?"

"Ten feet, sir," the Navigating officer replied as he read off the trace from the revolving pointer on the electrical sounding-machine, a gadget that indicated the depth under the keel.

"Give it every half-minute, please; I don't think I can go much further."

"Aye, aye, sir," replied Benson, more at ease with his instrument than with the trimming which Taggart was carrying out at this instant.

Through the periscope over which he slouched, the Captain watched the day draw rapidly to its close, a golden bronze stealing gloriously across the western horizon. Then to the southward a smattering of white buildings showed, a long pier jutting out into the sea like a man's finger.

"Bearing of the pier, THAT."

"Right ahead, sir."

"Course?"

"One-eight-o, sir."

So they were right on their D.R., a mile and a half north of the only pier.

"I don't dare go any further in," Joe murmured, "or an aircraft might spot us in these shallows. Take her down slowly until we bottom."

"Aye, aye, sir." Taggart's young face concentrated on taking the boat gently to the bottom and there was a gentle scraping along the hull.

"Stop starboard."

The telegraph tinkled and then there was the most delicious silence as U-679 lay stopped, grounded on the sandy bottom.

"Pass the word, Pilot" — Joe could not bring himself to address the Pilot as his First Lieutenant while Sinclair was away, for some deep superstitious reason perhaps — "pass the word that I will be surfacing as soon as it's dark, at about nine o'clock, and that we shall have to look sharp if we are to take off the shore party."

"Second Cox'n!"

Joe scratched his head quizzically as he addressed the Second Cox'n, the black-bearded giant on the fore-planes who was awaiting the order to dismiss.

"Sir?"

"When I surface I shall remain trimmed right down, but I shall want you and one seaman on the fore-casing to cope with any eventualities should the shore party arrive in a hurry."

"Aye, aye, sir. Shall I take heaving lines?"

"Yes, a couple," and he turned to Goddard, the signalman whose slight build belied the strength of character lying behind the imperturbable veneer.

"Signalman?"

"Sir."

"Have the infrared Aldis ready."

"Aye, aye, sir."

So, all preparations made, U-679 lay silently on the bottom, a mile and a half from Sidi Barrani, waiting for the hands of the clock to creep round to nine. The men fed and then slept fitfully while they waited, strung to a high nervous tension as they realised the gravity of the situation.

Almost certainly the enemy must have stumbled upon something by now and be hounding the shore party. Even if

Peter and Jan reached the port, how were they to come off? And suppose enemy destroyers suddenly appeared again, as they did in Mersa Matruh? All these doubts flashed through the minds of those on board, for the lives of three of their own depended upon the next few hours, and men were silent as they waited.

"Nine o'clock, sir," Taggart reported round the Ward Room screen.

"Very good, Sub. Go to Diving Stations."

So, in the first hour of darkness, U-679 slithered silently to the surface where she wallowed not far from the pier, unseen in the low visibility that had drifted in from the coast.

As Joe peered through his glasses, he had a sensation of nervousness which he had never experienced before, an ominous feeling of disaster difficult to explain. The mist curled around them in trailing fingers to reduce the visibility to less than half a mile.

"At last, a bit of luck," Joe sighed to himself, "but it will be almost impossible for anyone to find us in this stuff, including Number One, Jan and Hawkins," and he removed his binoculars momentarily to ease his stinging eyes.

"Better get the infrared Aldis up, Signalman, and start flashing all round, though they won't see much in this."

"Aye, aye, sir."

Goddard dipped into the conning tower to plug in the Aldis and then, unwinding the long lead behind him, he re-emerged to perch himself at the after-end of the bridge where he shipped the dark red infrared glass. Then, tap-tapping on the trigger, he patiently swept the horizon full circle with long flashes invisible to the human eye.

Nine-thirty. Joe looked at his watch and grunted to Taggart who stood beside him, eyes glued to his binoculars.

"Not much chance in this, Sub."

"No, sir, I don't like this haze. You can't distinguish the shoreline from the horizon, and the strain makes one's eyes ache so."

Joe turned round and saw Goddard passing a tired hand across his forehead.

"Better take tricks on that job, Signalman. I'll get the P.O. Tel. up to relieve you for half an hour."

"Thank you, sir."

Close on the heels of Petty Officer Haig, the P.O. Tel., there followed Able Seaman Bowles who clambered up to relieve the port lookout, and then the quiet of the concentrating watch was resumed. Joe was restless, his nerves frayed and on edge. By great good fortune they had managed to make the rendezvous, but so much could have gone wrong at the shore-end. Supposing Hawkins had never contacted Sinclair? The horror of their probable fate flashed across his mind, and he swore softly to himself. Without his trusted First Lieutenant he felt insecure, and the added strain of having to keep a closer eye on his officers was beginning to tell now that Sinclair was ashore. And then there was this visibility — if it didn't clear soon Sinclair and his party would never find them.

"Red one-two-o, sir," Bowles shouted excitedly, his eyes glued to his binoculars.

"What, for Pete's sake?" Joe snapped, as he spun round to stand directly behind Bowles, his glasses instinctively lining up on the same bearing.

"Looks like a U-boat, sir, coming straight towards. She's growing larger, sir."

Joe leapt for the klaxon push.

"Clear the bridge, dive, dive, dive!" he yelled frantically.

The lookouts bundled swiftly through the hatch, followed by the P.O. Tel. with the Aldis, the long flex trailing behind him.

"Quick, Haig, she's almost on top of us!"

The P.O. Tel. dropped into the void, while Joe stood impatiently on the lip of the hatch, waiting to jump down on top of him. But the man's head remained in the aperture and he seemed to be fumbling at something with his hands.

"The lead is snarled up around the hatch clips, sir," Haig yelled desperately, "I'm trying to clear it."

"For God's sake, get a move on, she's almost on top of us!"

Joe danced impotently upon alternate feet, while the approaching U-boat bore down blindly upon them.

"She can't see us, or she would have torpedoed us by now," Joe whispered to himself as the conning tower of the oncoming U-boat grew into the size of a house. He could already see the white teeth at her bows as she ploughed remorselessly towards them, now barely two hundred yards off.

In the darkness, Haig's hands tore at the knotted flex, wound inextricably around the long handle of the clips. "Keep calm," he was muttering to himself, "don't panic — the only way to get this clear is to work methodically," and he forced his brain to memorise the complicated loops of the infernal muddle. He shoved the lead nearest the handle of the Aldis into his mouth, and while it hung suspended by his teeth, he arched his back against the tower with all his might, his feet slipping on the oily rungs of the ladder.

"For God's sake, Haig, let me down, the water's at bridge level!" Joe yelled desperately as the diving boat started to slide beneath the sea.

"Got it, sir!" Haig shouted, as he wrenched the last coil free and the flex whipped through the hatch, "you can shut the lid now!"

Joe jumped into the black void, but as he did so he caught a glimpse of the scything bows and conning tower of the U-boat which now lunged above them, poised to rip them asunder.

"She'll probably ram us in the after-ends," Joe whispered as he dragged the conning tower hatch shut over his head, the incoming sea drenching him with a sheet of water. "Well, we've tried our best," and then he heard the drumming of the propellers which threshed towards them. From the silence of the conning tower he could hear only Haig below him, panting from his frantic efforts. The lower conning tower hatch had been slammed shut beneath them by the Control Room, because they had presumed the upper lid to be still open when the water had cascaded down. And, in their steel coffin in the conning tower, Joe and the P.O. Tel. waited in the blackness for the impending crash that would put an end to them all in one overwhelming holocaust.

Then suddenly the lower hatch opened and the two trapped men slithered down in a heap.

"Depth?" Joe gasped, his eyes searching the gauges desperately.

"Thirty-five feet, sir."

The roar of the venting air from 'Q' tank added to the pandemonium, but now, even above this din, the pounding of the whirling propellers overhead overwhelmed everything.

Thirty-eight feet — thirty-nine — surely the disaster must swamp them now, mercifully, suddenly?

Benson had guessed something of what was happening and had instinctively shut all watertight doors, so that each compartment was sealed off from its neighbour, and in each steel tomb, men held their breaths and waited with upturned eyes, glassy eyes that clung to life's last few seconds before catastrophe deluged upon them.

"She's over the after-ends now," Joe spoke out loud, whilst the horror of the threshing propellers obliterated all else. "Here it comes…" and he shut his eyes to stop the dreadful picture that smothered his imagination.

And then it was gone, over and away, down the starboard side and out across the starboard bow, disappearing quickly into the distance.

For what must have been five full seconds, no one spoke nor moved, rooted to the spot, immovable statues of humanity, once more delivered from a horrible death by the Almighty. Then gradually into their consciousness drifted the familiar sounds of whining pumps and motors and they knew that they were safe.

Joe turned his face towards Benson, and the gaunt face creased into a slow smile.

"Don't think they even knew we were there, Pilot."

"Hope not, sir, or they'll be back."

"Have to chance that, for we must be up top to pick up Number One and his party," he said. "Stand by to surface."

"Stand by to surface, sir."

Then, a few seconds later, U-679 rose silently from the bottom to wait once more on the surface for the lone fugitives ashore. Joe looked at his watch: only nine forty-five! That had been the longest fifteen minutes in his life. But he sighed with relief when he saw that the visibility had already improved, so that he could just distinguish the loom of the buildings ashore.

"Signalman, get your perishing infrared going again," he ordered jocularly, "but, for Pete's sake see that the flex is clear for immediate dismantling this time. You nearly drowned your Captain!"

Goddard laughed in the darkness as his fingers crooked once more round the trigger — there would be no mistake this time.

In the darkness, trimmed right down with her fore-casing barely awash, U-679 weaved silently on her main motors, waiting off the pier for the fugitives, risking her very existence while she offered the only chance left to the men ashore who might not even be alive. Perhaps they had already put off from the shore and missed the submarine in the darkness? There were only seven hours left before dawn.

CHAPTER 24

The Flicker of the Guns

An hour after the last rays of the sun had splashed blood-red the whitewashed hovels, two detached soldiers of the Afrika Korps slipped quietly into the darkened street. They marched silently in step, but their course took them down the less populated alleys and they always seemed to keep in the shadows. Twice they nearly collided with a Security patrol, but on each occasion they paused to allow the patrol to pass by them.

"Only needs a wrong meeting now, Bill, and it'll be all up with us."

They came to the main street, a broad metalled road with a few shops lining the filthy gutters. An Arab brushed by them, and, as Peter stood back, he could just see the length of the shopping centre, now completely dark and deserted.

"Now, Bill!" he hissed as he started to streak across the road, and then, Bill close on his heels, he vanished down a squalid alleyway.

'Rue du Quai,' Peter glimpsed from the name plate at the corner. So this was it, at last! It could only be a few hundred yards to the harbour.

"*Achtung!* Who goes there?"

Peter and Bill froze in their tracks as the brilliant beam of a torch focused upon them, dazzling in the darkness.

"Advance and be recognised — one at a time."

Peter slowly advanced towards the beam, his heart thumping with the sudden shock, his left hand itching to reach for his

Luger which clung so comfortingly to his side. He dared not make a move for he could not see his challenger.

"Advance, number two!" and, a minute later, Peter felt Bill by his side.

"What unit are you from?" an ice-cold voice rasped and then, when the torch was lowered, Peter could make out the patrol of a sergeant and two privates neatly turned out in the distinctive dress of the S.S.

"Both from Transport, sergeant," and then Peter had a brilliant idea, one of those moments when the brain reacts with abnormally swift decision under stress.

"We were on sick leave, but we've been sent out by our platoon commander."

The suspicious sergeant was not convinced.

"What for?"

"To search for some supposed escaped Englishmen — spies, I think he said they were…"

The S.S. sergeant relaxed but laughed unpleasantly.

"And so you think you'll find them? Which way did they go, eh, answer me that?"

"Well, sergeant, our other two mates saw two suspicious men up there, and we were just going to investigate," and Peter pointed in the direction from whence they had come, the southern quarter of the town. "Would you like help?" and Peter grinned.

"No!" the sergeant exploded. "The S.S. don't need help from two privates in Transport. We'll find them our way. Come on!" and he jerked his head for his two companions to follow. As Peter watched the beam of the torch receding in the darkness, he sighed deeply.

"Phew! A near one, sir," Bill blurted. "Thank God it was the S.S. or the two privates would have wanted to talk with me!"

Peter was already disappearing down the alley, so that Bill had to lengthen his stride to keep up with him. They could now hear the surf breaking upon the beach and the noise was music in their ears. The alley led straight into the dock road, and there before them was the little harbour, a jumble of muddle and confusion. A low wall protected the street from the sea, while to the left the long jetty ran out towards the sea like a finger. Apart from the usual confusion of small huts and several small cranes, there was little else in the harbour, but then Peter saw what he was looking for — the small boat pound.

"There, Bill!"

At last they were nearly there! All they had to do was to commandeer a small boat and slip out to sea in this low visibility. And then they might contact U-679 if she was there…

Two big 'ifs'! Peter thought as he slipped past the wall. "Come on, Bill."

Peter glanced at his watch as he strode quietly down the trellised pier, which was a wooden, ramshackle affair of considerable length. It was glorious to see the water lapping blackly against the pier and to sniff the old smells of the sea.

"Look out, sir," Bill hissed, "there's someone coming down the jetty," and he leapt for cover behind two wooden crates on the dockside, while Peter continued to amble nonchalantly towards the noise of approaching footsteps.

"There are two of 'em, Bill. Stand by!"

From the blackness two figures loomed, one a huge man in S.S. uniform, the other of slighter build, and they both hurried past as they saw Peter, their faces averted. But Peter's hand loosened its hold on his pistol as he recognised the couple —

Jan Widdecombe and his prisoner, Kapitan Ulrich von Kramer!

"Jan!" Peter hissed at the backs which were now receding in the darkness.

Jan spun round, his hand still clutching his knife, for this was a moment of opportunity for his prisoner.

"Peter!"

The two men grinned foolishly at each other in the darkness, then Bill emerged sheepishly to join the party.

"Hullo, Bill," Jan whispered, "so you couldn't keep away!"

"Couldn't leave 'Jimmy-the-One', sir!"

Peter chuckled but there was little time for conversation pieces.

"Come behind these crates to talk — look out, he's escaping!" and Peter reached for his gun.

"Don't shoot!" Jan hissed, and within five bounds he was within reach of the disappearing Kramer. He hurled himself at the German's legs, tackling him low and bringing him down hard.

Peter heard the crash and the wind being knocked out of Kramer's barrel of a chest, then Jan's subdued oaths as he tried to grapple with the winded giant. Peter rushed to the noise in the darkness, drawing his Luger as he went; he found the crazed German sitting astride his opponent, with strong fingers already squeezing Jan's throat.

"Get up or I shoot!" Peter rapped in Kramer's ear as he jabbed the barrel into the small of Kramer's back. The sudden pain brought the brute to his senses and he relaxed his hold to glare furiously at Peter.

"Get up and hold your hands above your head!" and once more Peter dug the barrel into the man. "Now walk to those crates."

The German had almost lost control of himself, but now that his desperate bid for freedom had failed, he was like a pricked balloon, flabby and useless.

"Thanks, Peter, he almost had me," and Jan rubbed his bruised neck ruefully. "Better shoot him out of hand next time, even though the noise may give us away."

"Tie him up, Bill, and gag the blighter," Peter rapped out.

"Yes, sir — it'll be a pleasure!" and Bill wrenched Kramer's arms behind his back, while Peter covered him with the Luger. Then Peter beckoned Jan to follow him behind the crates, and they sat hunched upon their haunches while they waited for Bill to finish securing Kramer to the enormous packing cases. Soon Bill rejoined them, a satisfied smirk upon his face.

"He won't move far, sir," he chuckled.

"Good, Bill!" Peter replied. "Come and join the merry party!"

"The place is stiff with patrols and soldiers, Peter," Jan began. "I think they suspect something because that devil there" — and he jerked his head towards the gagged Kramer — "tipped off a driver who escaped. When we last saw him he was belting away to the east."

"Was he a lone driver with an ugly scar on his cheek?"

"Yes, that's right, but…"

"We had to kill him when we discovered accidentally that he'd bowled you out — a bit of luck for us!"

"But we wanted his truck," Bill grinned, "and he wouldn't oblige, so we had to take it."

So the story was pieced together, and it seemed that at least the grand deception plan was safe for the six-wheeler could have been the only suspicious element, and it had failed to keep track of Peter and Bill.

"Well, all that remains is to contact U-679, then," Jan said.

"Sounds easy, but what in?" asked Peter.

"There's a small pulling-boat at the inboard end of this pier, sir, but it would hardly take three," said Bill.

Peter and Jan eyed each other, as they realised that one of them would have to remain behind.

"You go, Jan, and take Bill," said Peter quietly.

"Don't be so stupid," Jan rapped angrily. "I can look after myself, but you can't. You go."

Jan grunted.

"This isn't getting us very far, is it? Now I suppose Hawkins wants to be left behind!"

"Not on your flippin' life, sir, but I ain't goin' without you two officers, and that's flat!"

Peter chuckled.

"That's mutiny, Able Seaman Hawkins!"

"Don't mind what it is, sir, but I ain't leaving you two."

Peter looked at his watch. Ten-fifteen.

"Well, we'd better get a move on. If Joe's there, he'll be looking for us soon," Peter continued. "Did you bring the infrared glass with you, Bill?"

"Yes, sir. I've saved it in me wallet, and I reckon there's enough of it left to see through."

Jan had been strangely silent, and then he suddenly interrupted.

"Wait a minute, Peter, I saw several air-sea-rescue launches at the end of the pier. But there were two sentries…"

Peter had stiffened and stood up suddenly, as from the dock road there came the rhythmic sound of marching feet.

"Come on, chaps! Let's get moving; I have a hunch someone's looking for us. We'll rush the guard, get on board the outboard launch and make a dash for it."

"What about Kramer?" Jan snapped.

"Bring him, Bill," Peter ordered. "I'll lead on, Jan — you bring up the rear."

"Aye, aye, sir," Bill chuckled, his knife flashing in the darkness as he slashed at Kramer's bonds. "I'd rather have a bullet through my head than wait to be captured by this lot," and he nodded towards the town.

Jan agreed as he helped to force Kramer to his feet. They ripped the gag from his face and loosed his arms.

"Now, Kramer," Peter rapped, "get on in front of me and persuade the launch to take us off. I'm just behind you."

Kramer stood his ground for a split second, and then Peter's thumb slipped off the safety catch of his Luger.

"Might as well shoot you now then, if you won't help — you would have shot Harry Arkwright out of hand in Castellare Poliano," he added. "We have nothing to lose now. Are you going or not? We've no time to waste."

Kramer stood fascinated by the gun barrel which was aimed directly at his heart.

"I'll go," he gasped hoarsely.

"Get weaving! They're near the gates now!" Bill whispered.

With Kramer leading the way, they all loped quietly down the pier, and then they saw the line of launches, four abreast, alongside the seaward end of the jetty. Suddenly two figures lumbered towards them from out of the darkness.

"*Achtung!* Halt or I fire," a querulous voice challenged.

"Now, Kramer, do your stuff, or else—" and Peter jabbed the gun into the man's back.

"Kommandant Kramer of the S.S.," Kramer shouted, "I wish to take these three men with me to the outboard boat."

The guard paused, and, with a feeling of intense relief, Peter saw him begin to lower his rifle. Then his companion's eyes lighted for a moment upon Jan and he leapt towards him, yelling at the top of his voice, "*Achtung!* The spies! The…"

Four orange flames spurted in the darkness, and Peter felt the Luger jumping in his hand. The nearest sentry spun round as the lead hit him and then he crumpled and slid silently over the sill of the jetty. There was a distant splash from the water below.

His companion doubled up and sank to the jetty with a look of horror frozen on his face. From behind, Peter heard the steps of marching men reaching the entrance to the pier, and then quickly, much too quickly, the noise grew louder.

"Get going, Kramer!" and Peter's smoking gun prodded him down the sloping gangway. Slithering and sliding, they jumped on to the first launch, and then Peter pushed ahead to leap across the boats until he reached the outboard vessel. The inboard launches seemed to be unmanned, and it was obvious that the outboard launch was the Duty Boat for the night, because startled faces began to appear at the hatchway when the Englishmen's footsteps pounded upon the decks.

"Take the Engine Room, Jan!" Peter yelled. "Get the engines going! We'll deal with the rest."

Jan jumped at the mechanic who stood transfixed by surprise in the hatchway of the Engine Room. The blade of Jan's knife gleamed and the man disappeared below.

"Down below, all of you!" Peter shouted in German at the first figures who were trying to shoulder their way out of the for'd hatch. "Come on, Kramer — get below! Shut the hatch on them, Bill!" and Peter fired a random shot at the hatch. There was a flurry and the faces disappeared, Kramer jumping on top of them. Bill banged the hatch-cover sheet and threw the samson bar across to batten them down and trap them in their own fo'c'sle.

"Let go, Bill!" Peter yelled in anguish as he heard running footsteps upon the pier. "I'll slip aft!"

Peter dashed to the stern rope, and, as he fumbled to let it go, he realised that the engines were silent.

"Oh, God!" he groaned, "what's up with the engines?"

Were they to be caught now, at the very last moment? But, as he leapt for'd, the engines spluttered, coughed a moment, and then roared into life.

"Full ahead together!" Peter yelled into the din of the engine room hatch as he dashed past. "Cut everything, Bill!" he shouted to the fo'c'sle. "Bear off and stand clear!"

The first bullet smacked against the bridge side. Then all hell was let loose as the rifle-fire crackled with orange flashes from the jetty.

"All gone for'd, sir!" Bill shouted, as he hurled himself to the deck and crawled to the starboard side of the bridge.

"Take cover!" Peter warned as the launch surged ahead under full power to draw away from her next-door neighbour. But it seemed slow, agonisingly slow, for now the marksmen were much more accurate as a searchlight flashed on to sweep the harbour from the pier head.

The launch was gathering way, her wake frothing at her stern, when the beam caught her.

"Down all of you!" Peter cried above the pandemonium. "Keep your hats on!" and he felt the boat surge forward, when a sudden pain stabbed his left thigh.

I'm hit! he thought, and then he actually found himself laughing as he coaxed the launch out of the harbour mouth. Keeping close to the piles and directly under the searchlight beam, so that the light could not depress sufficiently to reach them, they were soon once more plunged into darkness.

Then suddenly, out of the mantle of invisibility, the cruel beam of the searchlight caught them. As they swept past, barely fifty feet from the light, Jan, who was crouching at the entrance of the engine room hatch, deliberately emptied his revolver at the glass. On the fifth shot, the lamp shivered and went out, while bullets whined overhead.

"Well done, Jan!" Peter sang out exultantly, "well done, my boy-o!" and he swung the wheel over, first to port, then to starboard, so that she weaved away from the entrance while the bullets whistled harmlessly away to starboard. Peter took her straight out into the night.

"Reckon we must be about a mile out by now, Peter," Jan yelled from aft. "She ought to be about here."

Peter reduced speed, and in the sudden quiet, all he could hear was the whisper of the breeze as the speed came off her. Peter's eyes ached as he stared ahead. Bill stood by him, peering desperately through the infrared glass while he swept the horizon.

"She may never have got here, Jan," Peter shouted anxiously.

"Well, she'd better show up, if she's to be here at all," Jan yelled from the engine room hatch. "I can hear the other launches starting up."

And then, above the faint swish of their bow wave, as they cut slowly through the water, the faint roar of engines thrummed in Peter's ears. He looked round and then stiffened. Were those a couple of bow waves that he could see already?

"There she is, sir! There she is!" Bill shouted hysterically. "Look, sir, look! Red four-o, flashing red light!" and his shaking hand stretched out to port.

Peter swung the wheel over.

"Con me on, Bill — I can't see her!"

As the boat's bows swung across the bearing, Bill's arm was pointing directly over the bows.

"*There*, sir, you're right on — *now* — no, a bit more to starboard ... *now*, sir, you're on!"

Peter glanced at his ship's head and steadied on the bearing, but from astern the roar of the pursuers was ominously loud.

Suddenly from out of the darkness a huge square shape loomed above them.

"Hard-a-port, sir, hard-a-port!" Bill screamed, "you'll hit her..." and then, as the launch swung crazily to port, her quarter swung out and crashed against the U-boat's pressure hull. There was a splintering crash. Then the launch bounced and slithered down the black side, her guard rails and deck fittings shearing off like butter as she did so. On the fo'c'sle, the fore-hatch burst open with the shock.

"Jump for it!" Peter yelled. "Jump!" and, as he leapt from the bridge, he saw Bill scrambling on to the U-boat's gun-sponson. Jan leapt across the space of water to land on the fore-casing, where he fell and slithered to a stop on the edge.

The launch had bounced clear when Peter jumped. He knew he could not make the distance when he was in mid-air, and then he hit the water.

Idiot! he cursed to himself, *what do you want to drown for now?* and he looked up to see the face of a fiend leaning over the stern of the disappearing wreck of a launch. Kramer, who had burst through the shattered fore-hatch, was shaking a clenched fist and shouting hysterically. Peter just caught his words when a heaving line plopped across his reeling head.

"You young puppy — I'll get you yet! Yes, I'll kill you with my own hands one day!" and the lunatic voice became unintelligible in the distance.

"Hold on, sir, I'll heave you up."

The second cox'n lugged him from the water, and, as he scrambled up the side of the conning tower, he caught sight of four white bow waves barely four hundred yards away.

"Dive, dive, dive!"

The dreamlike quality of Joe's command seemed unreal as the klaxon roared and the bridge was cleared. Dark figures leapt past him in the darkness.

Peter stood transfixed alongside Jan. They both stood staring at the eastern horizon.

As the water started to splash round their feet, the Captain's voice snapped angrily.

"Get below — we're diving! What are you looking at, for Pete's sake?"

The two men turned round, the thread of wonder still unbroken as they smiled jubilantly at their Captain.

"Look, sir! Look all along the desert horizon!"

The eastern sky was alive with flickering flashes of light. The guns of Alamein were speaking at last.

EPILOGUE

The sandstone balcony of Lazaretto was packed with cheering men when H.M. Submarine U-679 secured alongside, her Jolly Roger flapping proudly at her for'd periscope, and her White Ensign dazzlingly bright in the sunlight.

The burly figure of Captain 'S' was almost on the same level as Joe Croxton who leant happily across the bridge rail, having rung off main engines.

"Nice to have you back, Joe!"

"Good to be here, sir, particularly with the party all complete."

'S' smiled with contentment.

"But I'm afraid I've got to split your team up again."

There was a long pause as Joe looked round at his officers who were grouped behind him on the bridge: Jan Widdecombe, the valiant Commando; Ian Taggart, the impetuous Sub; Benson, his trusted pilot; and then Peter Sinclair, his loyal Number One who had just finished supervising the wire hawsers…

"Split us up, sir?"

"Yes. Lieutenant Sinclair is flying home tomorrow in a Dakota for his C.O.Q.C."

Joe turned towards Peter.

"Hear that, Number One? You're flying home tomorrow for your 'perisher'!"

Peter could not believe his ears.

"Me, sir?" he murmured incredulously, "for my 'perisher'?"

The loud voice of Captain 'S' bellowed from the balcony.

"D'you think you can be ready in time, Sinclair?"

Peter reached the bridge side.

"You bet I can, sir!" and he grinned, while the others slapped him on the back.

He just could not credit the fact! Tomorrow he would be flying home to take his Commanding Officers Qualifying Course in England. If he were successful he would soon be Captain of his own submarine!

He heard a hoarse cough at his elbow and he looked round. Joe Croxton's smouldering eyes met his as they shook hands.

"Congratulations, Number One, and keep your temper when you are a C.O.! Thank you for everything."

Peter could not speak as he felt the pressure of the strong hand. Instead he turned away and disappeared rapidly down the conning tower hatch.

GLOSSARY

ASDIC — The device by which submarines are detected. Submarines are also fitted with this device, when it is used as a hydrophone.

BEARING — The direction of an object.

BLOWERS — Machines with which to blow out the water in the tanks by using low-pressure air.

CORTICENE — A type of heavy linoleum used to cover the steel deck.

CRACK — To open a valve quickly, and to shut it again immediately.

E-BOAT — The fast enemy motor torpedo boat.

E.T.A. — Expected Time of Arrival.

FOCKE-WOLFE — German long-range reconnaissance aircraft.

FREE FLOOD — The open holes in the casing and tanks through which the water enters.

FRUIT MACHINE —A metal box into which all relevant attack data is fed, and from which the necessary information is extracted with which to carry out an attack.

GROUP DOWN — Low speed on the main electric motors, thus using up little electric power.

GROUP UP — High speed on the main electric motors, thus using up the battery power quickly.

H.E. — High Explosive.

H.E. — Hydrophone Effect, i.e. propeller noise.

HEAT — Slang for a submarine at the receiving end of a severe depth-charge attack.

H.P. — High Pressure.

H.S.D. — Higher Submarine Detector; the rank of a skilled Asdic operator.

HYDROPHONE — Underwater listening device.

JIMMY-THE-ONE — Slang for First Lieutenant.

JOLLY ROGER — Skull-and-crossbones flag, upon which emblems of sinkings are sewn. Flown to denote successes.

LAYER — A difference of temperature gradients in the ocean.

MAIN BALLAST KINGSTON — Water into the internal tanks amidships is allowed to enter through the Kingston Valves.

MAIN BALLAST TANKS — The tanks which give a submarine its buoyancy. All are fitted with main vents, numbers 1 and 6 being external, the remainder internal.

MAIN VENTS — The large mushroom valves on top of the Main Ballast tanks. When the main vents are open, the water will rush into the tanks, but, if the main vents are shut, the air cannot escape when the Main Ballast tanks are blown, because the 'blow' is at the top of the tank and the free-flood holes at the bottom. Water is therefore forced out through the holes in the bottom of the tank, H.P. air taking its place.

MESSERSCHMITT — ME109; single-seater German fighter.

OUTSIDE E.R.A. — The Engine Room Artificer whose duty is at the panel in the Control Room, and who is therefore 'outside' the Engine Room.

PANEL — The conglomeration of valves, etc., all centralised at one position.

PERISHER — Slang for Commanding Officers' Qualifying Course.

'Q' TANK — The emergency tank for quick diving. When flooded, the tank makes the submarine ten tons heavier than her normal dived trim. After diving, this extra water is blown out of 'Q' tank by high-pressure air. If this tank is required to be flooded when dived, its vent has merely to be opened, either into the submarine or outboard, and the sea will rush into 'Q' tank. In wartime, for obvious reasons, 'Q' tank is always kept flooded when the submarine is on the surface.

STICK — Slang for 'periscope'.

THIRD HAND — The Third Officer in a submarine.

U-BOAT — Enemy submarine.

URSULA SUIT — Waterproof overalls in general use, designed by the Commanding Officer of H.M. Submarine *Ursula*.

WIMPEY —Wellington medium bomber, British.

WOP — Slang for 'Italian'.

A NOTE TO THE READER

Dear Reader,

If you have enjoyed the novel enough to leave a review on **Amazon** and **Goodreads**, then we would be truly grateful.

Sapere Books is an exciting new publisher of brilliant fiction and popular history.

To find out more about our latest releases and our monthly bargain books visit our website:
saperebooks.com